PRAISE FOR
SCRITCH SCRATCH

"A teeth-chattering, eyes bulging, shuddering-and-shaking, chills-at-the-back-of-your-neck ghost story. I loved it!"

— R. L. Stine, author of the Goosebumps series

"A spine-tingling blend of hauntings and history."

— *Publishers Weekly*

"*Scritch Scratch* brims with eerie thrills and nail-biting chills that are sure to keep readers turning pages. Don't dare read this at night!"

— Kate Hannigan, author of *Cape*, book one in The League of Secret Heroes series

"Delightfully chilling and rooted in history, this haunting thrill ride will keep you hooked."

— Jess Keating, author of *Nikki Tesla and the Ferret-Proof Death Ray*

"Mary Downing Hahn fans will enjoy this just-right blend of history and spooky."

— *Kirkus Reviews*

"A scary tale that lives up to the reputation of haunted Chicago... offers a ghost-hunterly blend of reality and chills that should appeal to many readers with creepy interests."

— *The Bulletin of the Center for Children's Books*

"Delightfully chilling and rooted in history, this haunting thrill ride will keep you hooked."

— Jarrett Lerner, author of the EngiNerds series

PRAISE FOR
WHAT LIVES IN THE WOODS

"Currie...throws all the frightfully fun trappings of haunted house tales at readers, who will soak up the stormy nights, town rumors, exploding light bulbs, creeping shadows, unsettling whispers...light horror for larger collections."

—*Booklist*

"A perfect middle-grade horror selection...holds its own as a shivery standalone."

—*The Bulletin of the Center for Children's Books*

"The scares are real, the resolution satisfying, and a sequel would be welcome...A thrilling read with an engaging protagonist."

—*Kirkus Reviews*

"An appropriately tween horror story in staccato chapters with plenty of goose bumps."

—*School Library Journal*

PRAISE FOR
THE PECULIAR INCIDENT ON SHADY STREET

"Give this page-turner to readers seeking a spooky thrill reminiscent of books by Mary Downing Hahn and filled with strong family relationships, budding friendships, a local history, mystery, and creepiness."

—*School Library Journal*

"Shivers aplenty; just the ticket for a cold autumn night."

—*Kirkus Reviews*

"A perfect flashlight read, Currie's debut is peppered with incidents that will make the reader's skin crawl and teeth chatter."

—*Booklist*

"This book has it all. Mystery, suspense, and lots of laughs."

—*TIME for Kids*

ALSO BY LINDSAY CURRIE

What Lives in the Woods

Scritch Scratch

The Peculiar Incident on Shady Street

THE GIRL IN WHITE

THE GIRL IN WHITE

LINDSAY CURRIE

sourcebooks
young readers

Published by Sourcebooks Young Readers, an imprint of Sourcebooks
P.O. Box 4410, Naperville, Illinois 60567–4410
(630) 961-3900
sourcebooks.com

Cataloging-in-Publication Data is on file with the Library of Congress.

This product conforms to all applicable CPSC and CPSIA standards.

Source of Production: Maple Press, York, Pennsylvania, United States
Date of Production: June 2022
Run Number: 5025509

Printed and bound in the United States of America.

MA 10 9 8 7 6 5 4 3 2 1

To my son, Ben.

Cheers to your kindness, your accomplishments,

and the amazing journey that lies ahead.

We are so proud of you!

Sweet Molly once lived in Eastport

Sweet Molly once loved the sea

Sweet Molly lost Liam to the shadows

Now Sweet Molly is coming for ye...

PROLOGUE

I shuffle the photos around my desk, sorting the ones I like most into a special pile. Our teacher assigned us this project over a week ago, but I'm just now deciding which images I want to turn in. It might seem like I've been procrastinating, but that's not it. I simply couldn't stop snapping pictures. This town really is beautiful. Picturesque harbors, turquoise water, and sunshine for days. If everyone who lived in Eastport wasn't so strange, I'd probably love it here.

I'm staring at a photo of a wave crashing over a cluster of craggy rocks nestled on the shoreline when it starts up...*the feeling*. I sit up straighter, too familiar with the goose bumps peppering my arms and legs. Deep down I know there isn't actually someone watching me, but it's hard to believe that when my heart is racing and a scream is lodged in my throat.

Suddenly, I'm sweating even though I left the window open, and the air rushing in is cold.

When I look back down at my photos, *she's* there. Standing on the rocks in the picture is the old woman. The woman from my nightmares. I let my eyes flutter closed and try to force her out of my head. It doesn't work. She clings to my mind like a nasty weed, her mottled green fingers reaching for me even when I try to block them out. White eyes. Wrinkled skin. Worn rags over jutting bones.

She's not real. She's not real. She's not real.

I repeat it over and over, willing myself to be brave. When I reopen my eyes, she's gone. The photo is exactly how it was when I took it, frothy greenish-blue water rushing against the sharp, rocky shoreline. No woman. I let my head tip back and gulp at the cool air. Tears sting at my eyelids.

Everyone has bad dreams, but not everyone has the same one almost every single night. Then again, not everyone lives in Eastport, Massachusetts. Otherwise known as the most cursed city in the USA.

Lucky me.

ONE

Today is October first. It barged in on a gust of chilly air with red and orange leaves on its heels. Morning fog settled over our narrow streets like a cold, wet blanket, and everyone—and I mean *everyone*—is already wearing their chunkiest sweaters. For most people I know, October isn't just the end of T-shirts and flip-flops; it's the beginning of the *best* month of the year. Halloween month. The time when Eastport comes to life.

I will *never* be one of those people.

The bell above the door dings again, signaling another customer. This time it's a man and woman. They rush in, wide-eyed. As usual, their cell phones are up and they're taking pictures before the door even fully shuts behind them. The woman snaps a few pictures of the fake cobwebs Mom strung around the counter, while the man takes a photo of one of the tombstone centerpieces on the table closest to him. Most people would just be digging their Halloween decorations out on October first. Not us. We have them out year-round. The whole town does.

I sigh and set my dish towel down then adjust the ghost-shaped apron tied around my waist. "Hi, welcome to The Hill. I'm Mallory. Can I get you a seat?"

The woman lowers her phone long enough to blink at me. I'm not great at guessing ages, but I think she's in her thirties. Maybe younger. She looks me up and down, clearly surprised to see a twelve-year-old greeting her. "Wow. You work here?"

"This is my parents' restaurant," I answer, doing my best to sound chipper even though this is my least favorite place to be on a Saturday morning. I'd rather be sleeping. Catching up on my Netflix bingeing. Getting a cavity filled. Well, maybe not that. The point is I'd rather be pretty much anywhere but here. "I help them out after school and on the weekends."

Snagging two menus off the counter, I lead them to a booth by the window. It's my favorite spot in the restaurant, the only table that seems to get any sunlight at all. Everywhere else always feels dim and draped in shadows—probably because Mom and Dad like it that way. It's *atmospheric*, they say. Just as I set the menus down on the table, the man clears his throat.

"Oh, um... We were hoping to be seated *in the back*." He

whispers this last part like it's some special secret between us. I bite my tongue to keep from telling him that everyone knows why they want to sit there. Everyone has heard the stories.

I pick their menus up and make my way to the back corner of our restaurant. Dropping them down on a new table, I force a smile to my face. "This is the only table I have left back here. Is it okay?"

They nod vigorously. The woman starts scanning the room right away, her blond curls bouncing and waving at me as she jerks her head from side to side. I'm about to walk away and let their waiter take over when she leans forward. There's a conspiratorial smile on her face. *Uh-oh.* I know that smile.

"So, is it true?"

Her eyes dart to the wall, then back to me. I take a deep breath and remind myself to stay calm. Stay professional, as Dad would say. It's hard though. I'm so tired of this question. Tired of the cameras, the whispers, and the tour groups. My own gaze bounces to the wall, my mind snagging on the hundreds of coffins that linger just beyond it.

"No. It's just a dumb urban leg—"

My answer is cut short by my mother. She sweeps in so fast I didn't even see her coming. Dropping her hands to my shoulders, she steers me away so fast I nearly trip over my own feet. "Mallory, Mallory. Don't be silly! Of course, it's true."

Mom leans over their table, mouth spread into a sinister smile. "It happened in this very room. Although the stories are different, they all share one thing."

"What's that?" the man asks. He's on the edge of his seat. They both are. I'm not surprised. This is why people come here. It's not my dad's homemade meat loaf and mashed potatoes or my mom's nearly famous cherry pie. It's the wall. The story. *The curse.*

"The casket burst through that very wall." Mom dramatically fans her hand out toward the wall a few feet behind them. It's the wall that separates our restaurant from Old Shallows Hill Cemetery. Legend has it, many years ago on a stormy October night, that very wall suddenly started cracking. It splintered and broke so badly that a hole opened up and dirt started rushing in, followed by...a casket. The casket slid right into the middle of the room when people were eating. And that's not the worst part. Legend also claims it opened. Locals *love* to gossip about the rotting, flesh-covered bones that reportedly scattered across the room, a few of them making their way all the way to the tabletops. According to one version of the story, a bone even landed in a bowl of clam chowder, and the woman eating it fainted dead away. *Gross.*

"No one knows who that poor soul was—the soul whose eternal rest was disturbed that fateful night." Mom pauses and walks from table to table. They're all listening now. Forks hover in midair, eyes track her every move. Yup. As usual, she has them mesmerized. "But we do know one thing."

Silence for at least five full seconds. That's how she does it. Hooks them. When Mom finally starts speaking again, a few of her customers jump.

"They're angry and looking for revenge," I've heard the words so many times that I mouth them along with her. So ridiculous. Not only is there zero proof that a casket ever crashed into our restaurant, but even if it did, so what? I don't see how that's any worse than a bird flying into the window or a car accident happening outside. I guess that's part of living in Eastport, though. According to the locals, everything bad that happens here can be linked to one curse or another.

"Revenge on anyone who steps foot on this land." Her sinister smile is back. "That means revenge on every one of you. Oh, did I mention that the entire staff who was working in the restaurant that fateful night died a gruesome, untimely death?"

A few gasps break the silence. The couple I seated immediately starts snapping pictures of the wall like it's something magical. It's not. It's just a plain old wall with some black-and-white photos of the dining room back when it was called The Roosevelt. But because this wall is the only thing standing between our dining room and the bodies buried in the hill on the other side of it, people are fascinated. Toss in the casket story and the restaurant is *always* busy. On the weekends, people are willing to wait over an hour for one of these tables, and my parents love it. Dad makes gravestone-shaped pancakes. Mom props napkins up on the tables like little ghosts.

It's bananas. We moved here because Mom said she wanted a change of pace. Dad said he wanted whatever Mom wanted. I think they just needed to get away from their problems in Chicago. Mom worked as an assistant at a law firm, and Dad worked at a bank. I heard them complain about work a lot back then. Bills too. They're careful not to talk about that stuff in front of me, but sometimes I wish they would. Then maybe I'd understand why they dragged me to a town held together by stupid legends and bought a restaurant everyone thinks is cursed.

I walk away in a huff as another camera flash goes off. A year and a half later, and I'm finally realizing the truth: the only thing that's cursed here in Eastport is *me*.

TWO

"Mallory," my father says, his scowl deepening. He wipes his hands down the front of his apron and beckons me into the kitchen. "Haven't we asked you not to do that?"

"I was just telling the truth," I mumble.

"Well, stop. You know better." He looks through the door at Mom, who now has everyone out of their seats and crowded around the window facing the graveyard, and smiles. "That legend is our bread and butter. It's why the restaurant is doing so well!"

He's not wrong. The Hill looks great now, but the first time I came here it was a dump. The people who owned it before us were so behind on their rent I guess they stopped fixing things that broke. The counters were dingy, the leather on the booths was cracked and patched, and the floors were chipped from one too many fumbled coffee mugs. Even the paint was peeling. I had no idea why my parents were interested in it. Before this, their idea of homemade dinners was those little meal kits the grocery store puts together—the ones that include all the ingredients *and* a recipe card. Then they suddenly wanted to move across the country and become restaurant owners?

So. Weird.

I blame my uncle Ricky. He's a real estate agent in a neighboring town. If he hadn't given my parents a sneak peek of this listing while we were here to visit him, none of this would've happened. I'd still be in Chicago, where people aren't obsessed with witches, and curses, and ghostly stuff. I wouldn't be living in a rental because we still can't afford a house. Oh, yeah…I'd also be sleeping right now, instead of wiping down crumb-covered tables.

"Plus, this is probably going to be our best month!" Dad exclaims. "You know how Eastport gets in October."

Unfortunately, I do. Eastport has a population of seven thousand people. But during the summer and fall, our most touristy months, that triples. Apparently, some big television show on the Travel Channel featured our town ten years ago. They called it "quaint, yet foreboding," and talked about how we have no less than seven graveyards within our city limits. They also brought up all the bizarre legends people tell around here. Everything from ghostly apparitions by the sea, to haunted lighthouses, and of course, coffins crashing through walls. It brings a lot of weirdos here. *Especially* in October.

"Look," Dad starts. "I understand this isn't exactly your cup of tea. But this place," he sweeps his hands out over the plates of steaming waffles and bacon waiting in the pickup window. "This place is paying the bills. It's also keeping you in those fancy sneakers you love so much."

Dad looks pointedly at my brand-new pair of Converse shoes. I really wish I hadn't worn them today.

"I just don't understand why we can't have a *normal* restaurant."

"What's normal?" he poses.

"I don't know. Maybe somewhere where Mom doesn't go full-on haunted house every day?" I toss my hands into the air, bringing them down just as Arthur, the restaurant souschef, walks by with a plate of Six-Feet-Under Scrambled Eggs. It crashes to the ground thunderously, drawing a few shrieks from the dining room.

Mom pops her head into the kitchen. She eyes the mess on the floor. After a moment of shock, she claps. "Well done! Sorry about the spill, of course, but your timing was perfect! I was just reenacting the casket crash and you two brilliantly provided the soundtrack!"

Leveling an *I told you so* look at Dad, I kick my feet out

one at a time to get the bits of scrambled eggs off my shoes. Mom rushes back out into the dining room. I'd like to think she's refilling coffee mugs, but I know better. She's weaving more stories. Dark ones.

Sigh. I don't know why I bother. There is no normal in Eastport.

Dad washes his hands and takes up his usual spot by the grill while I scoop up the eggs from the floor. "Look. Forget your shoe addiction. This restaurant is also keeping you at Harbor Point. You want to stay there, don't you?"

I look up at the mention of my school. Harbor Point is my favorite place. It's the only silver lining to living in Eastport. "You know I want to stay there. I worked hard to get in."

"Yes, you did," Dad says with a smile. "They would have been fools not to admit you. You're talented, Mal. Very talented. But fancy art schools aren't cheap."

I know what he's getting at. We never could have afforded a school like Harbor Point back in Chicago. We always had money for the stuff we needed, but there was never any extra. No fun dinners out, no limited-edition sneakers, and definitely no private art school where I can take photography classes. It took over a year for the restaurant to make enough money for us to afford it, but now that I'm finally there, I'm never looking back.

"I'm sorry," I say, my cheeks heating with guilt. I want to

be a travel photographer someday, visiting faraway countries and taking pictures of toucans and ruins and...well, anything other than the same old stuff here. Plastic cauldrons brimming with fake fog. Oversized spiders perched in lawns. Graveyards around every corner. Harbor Point is my way out. "I'll play along next time."

"Thank you." Dad cracks a few egg whites into a skillet but drops the yolks in a different bowl.

"What's that going to be?" I ask.

Dad pushes the edges of the egg around until it stays in a shape he's happy with. Then he uses a wooden spoon to hollow out two circles toward the top. Grabbing the bowl off the counter, he gently sets one yolk in each circle. They look like bright yellow eyes popping out of a...

"Sunny-Side Up Skull!" He announces, sliding the eggs onto a plate and holding it out proudly. I nod, too grossed out to do much else. Who in the world would want their breakfast to resemble a skull with gooey eyes? Just then, a burst of applause sounds from the dining room. I look out just in time to see Mom taking a dramatic bow with a large fake bone in her hand.

Mmmm-hmm. Maybe Dad's skull eggs are going to be more popular than I thought.

"Hey, why don't you get out of here? Go hang out with your friends for a while," Dad suggests.

Hope blooms inside me. I quickly crush it down. Saturdays are The Hill's busiest days. Last weekend, there was a line outside until almost two o'clock in the afternoon!

Dad catches my uncertainty and nudges me toward the door. "Go. Janette is coming in early today, so we'll be covered."

"But who will clean up the tables?" I ask.

"Mom."

"And the cash register? Who will take care of that?"

"Janette," Dad chuckles.

I cross my arms over my chest. It can't possibly be this easy. "Who will seat people?"

"Stop," Dad laughs. "Everything will be fine here. What I'm worried about are those dark circles under your eyes, kiddo. I think you need a day off, okay?"

He has no idea how true that is. I rush forward and give him a hug. "Thank you!"

"You got it. And chin up. Things might seem tough now, but remember that Dentons don't—"

"I know, I know. Dentons don't give up." I finish his sentence for him.

Peeling the apron off my waist, I wad it up and stuff it into my backpack. Time to get out of here before Dad changes his mind. Or worse, before Mom realizes what he's done.

THREE

I hit the sidewalk in a rush of adrenaline. Even though the skies are gray and a cold drizzle is falling, I couldn't be happier. This is the first Saturday in a looooong time that I haven't spent all day cooped up in the restaurant. I could call Emmie or Bri and go shopping. I could snap some pictures. I could take a walk or maybe even go to a movie. I could...

Sleep.

Just thinking about crawling into my warm and fluffy comforter makes me yawn. It has been a long time since I had a whole Saturday to myself and even longer since I got a good night of sleep. It's virtually impossible. When we first moved to Eastport, the dreams didn't happen as often. Maybe once a month. Now? They're pretty much every night. *All* night. Sometimes they're so vivid that it takes me hours to convince myself it wasn't real. That I'm safe. No wonder the skin under my eyes is always puffy and my friends keep asking if I'm okay.

"Mornin', Mallory!" Mrs. James waves from the doorway of the flower shop. She's a nice, older lady. Round and pink-cheeked even when it's cold outside. Today she's wearing a black T-shirt with a cauldron in the center. It reads *Eastport, MA. We'll put a spell on you.* Her wild white hair is covered by a baseball cap with a gravestone protruding from the top.

I pull a smile to my face. "Hi, Mrs. James."

"Got the day off work?" She waves some kind of garden tool in the air. It's pointy and pronged and looks more like a murder weapon than something she could use for potting. "C'mon in and I'll tell you all about the shadow that drifted down my hallway last night! It was positively terrifying!"

I nod and wave, hoping she'll think I can't hear her over the hum of cars on the street. I do *not* want to hear her story. People here are talkative. Too talkative. And it's never normal conversation either. It's always some strange story they're hoping will become popular enough to end up one of Eastport's newest legends. And Mrs. James's flower shop? No thank you. I like plants and all, but her shop isn't cheerful or flower-filled. It's grim. Cobwebs stand in the corners and chipped pots filled with scraggly weeds line the shelves. I wrinkle my nose up at the memory of the smell. Mom says it's just fertilizer, but the sour odor is so strong that it stays in your nose long after you leave.

I hurry down the street, desperate to get away before anyone else starts talking to me. Each store I pass is more decked out than the last. Black and orange ribbons are wound around the light posts, and gauzy ghosts hang from the tree branches. The square is decorated like a graveyard. Plastic tombstones stand in rows and a scattering of fake bones dot the grass. A huge banner that reads *Happy Anniversary* is stretched between two giant maple trees.

Ah. Right. I remember now. Dad said something about this October being extra-important because it's the anniversary of the first recorded Eastport legend...er, curse. You'd think the town would celebrate the day it was founded, but no. They celebrate the first curse instead.

Molly Flanders McMulligan Marshall, otherwise known as Sweet Molly, supposedly lived here over two hundred years ago. Her twin brother Liam was a ship captain on one of Eastport's largest fishing boats. He died at sea in a horrible storm, and Molly never got over it. Most folks around here believe the storm was already building when he was sent on that final fishing voyage and that Molly was the only person in town who protested. Everyone else said he'd be fine, that the barely scraping-by town couldn't do without the haul he was expected to bring back. But when he didn't return, Molly's fear turned into grief. Her sadness grew and grew until one day, legend claims she walked down to the lighthouse in her best white nightgown and vanished in the morning mist.

Everyone loved Sweet Molly, so her presumed death shook the people of Eastport to their core. But what shook them the hardest was the news that with her final breath, Molly had cursed the entire town for choosing their precious fishing trade over her brother's life.

I snort at the idea. First of all, how could anyone possibly know what Molly said with her final breath? And secondly, I've probably heard five different versions of this legend since moving here. Some say Molly drowned. Others say she disappeared before she even touched the water. They do all agree on one thing though—her spirit roams the coastline by the lighthouse late at night, and if you dare to cross paths with her, she'll drag you into a watery grave as revenge.

Not something I'd celebrate, but whatever. Sweet Molly is the centerpiece of the town's monthly parade down Gaunt Street. *The girl in white*. A different resident dresses up in a flowing gown with a face full of cheap white convenience store makeup, then dramatically makes the trek to the lighthouse where she vanishes. Really, she just ducks into the trees while folks *ooh* and *aah* like they don't know where she went.

Everyone follows, including my friends, my parents, and a super creepy old man who plays a piano on wheels with keys made of bone.

Keys made of bones. What kind of town owns such a thing? Seriously.

A breeze suddenly whips through the trees, startling me. It's cold...so cold I shiver. The gray sky is darkening, and an ominous rumble of thunder echoes across the water. Black clouds roll in from all directions, casting shadows that give me the chills. Then the feeling comes, the one I get every time I'm alone. It's the sensation of eyes on me, of being watched even when I can't see anyone. I hate it. Scanning the area, I sigh. Like usual, there's no one there. I shake off the feeling, wishing I could be back in Chicago for just one day. Just one afternoon to walk down the streets of my old neighborhood, where everyone would be minding their own business instead of trying to come up with new and more annoying ways to entertain tourists.

Thunder snaps again, this time louder than before. The clouds look especially dark floating against the light green of the water. I instinctively pull my camera out of my bag, remove the lens cap, and take a few photos. Who knows, they might come in handy for a project in the future.

I'm just about to start running so I don't get caught in the storm when I notice a frail-looking old woman hobbling along the dock. Is that our neighbor, Mrs. Barry? I take a few steps closer and narrow my eyes on her form. It has to be her.

Ugh. I have no idea why she's down here, but Mom would kill me if she found out I left her right before a huge storm. She's ninety-two years old and lives alone, but everyone in town pitches in and helps her with little stuff. Groceries, paying bills, getting around. And since I'm the only one here right now, it looks like I'm her helper today. So much for sleeping.

I jog toward Mrs. Barry. She's mumbling, pacing back and forth next to the water like she's looking for a lost item. Maybe she dropped something in the water? If she did, we'll never find it. The water is deeper than it looks by the docks.

"Mrs. Barry?" I call out. She doesn't turn around. Lightning cracks overhead. The sound is sharp and leaves my ears ringing. The trees jutting up all around me look gnarled now, creepy against the angry backdrop of clouds. Whoa. We need to get out of here quickly.

I pull to a stop right behind her. "Um, Mrs. Barry? I don't know if you've noticed, but it's going to storm, so I think maybe I should help you get home."

Silence.

"Mrs. Barry?" I repeat, this time a little louder. Maybe she has more trouble with her hearing than I thought.

She stops moving but doesn't answer. Odd. I wait a long few seconds, then gently lay a hand on her shoulder to get her attention.

Mrs. Barry turns around slowly. Her movements are jerky. Strange. It isn't until she's fully facing me that I see the one thing I'm positive I'll never forget as long as I live. *Her eyes.* They're completely white. No color. No pupils. Just...white.

FOUR

I smother a scream with my hand.

That is *not* Mrs. Barry.

"N-n-never mind," I stammer, easing backward. Losing my balance, I hit the ground. Hard. I scramble backward, stopping only when I crash into something. The fence. I've backed into the metal wire of the fence that lines both sides of the trail.

The woman's icy eyes stare at me, unblinking. Her face is a mass of wrinkles, and her breathing is ragged. Both craggy hands wind together in a worried knot, like the twisted branches of an old tree. As terrified as I am, I can't help but glance down at her clothing. The fabric hanging off her bony body is tattered. Actually, it's more like a bunch of dirty dish towels strung together than clothing.

"Where is it?" Her voice is hushed. There's something desperate about it. *Sad.*

I stare at my sneakers to avoid looking at her again. A shiver races up and down my spine as I replay the question in my mind. I should answer, but the words keep getting stuck behind my tongue.

"Where is it?" The woman repeats. Only this time she doesn't sound pleading. She sounds angry.

"I don't know what you mean," I answer hesitantly. My voice is shaking so hard that I sound like a cracked version of myself.

"WHERE IS IT?" She shrieks this time, the fury of her tone making the ground tremble. Dark veins snake across the whites of her eyes until they're completely black. Pitch black like a night on a country road. I'm so scared that I can barely breathe. If there was such a thing as a zombie apocalypse, this woman would definitely be leading it. And I... I would be hiding.

The wind lashes my cheeks, whips my hair around, and tugs at me. It's dragging me toward the woman, but I don't want to go.

My feet skid across the wooden planks. I reach out for something, *anything*, that might be able to stop her from pulling me closer. Finally catching the edge of a railing, I hold on as tight as I can. Lightning streaks across the darkened sky, illuminating the old woman's face. It's pale except for the inky pools of black swimming where her blank eyes used to be.

"Leave me alone!" I scream. I tighten my grip on the railing I'm clinging to. Sharp pieces of wood dig into my fingers, but I don't care. Squeezing my eyes shut tight, I try to imagine that she's walking away. Maybe if I think about it hard enough, it will happen.

Please go away. Please go away. Please go away.

In an instant, I'm on the ground, grasping and clawing. I lick my lips, suddenly aware of a terrible taste in my mouth. Dirt.

"Honey, are you okay? Can I call someone for you?" A blond woman with a stroller is staring down at me. Her forehead is wrinkled up in concern.

I shake my head. The old woman is only a few feet away. She's hunched over, still lumbering slowly along the path.

"Her. She did this!" I jab a shaky finger in her direction.

The woman stops walking and turns around.

My jaw drops. It's *not* the same woman. Not even close. The zombie woman had sagging skin, wild eyes, and torn clothing. This woman is old but normal-looking. She's got gray hair and a warm smile. Her clothes aren't ripped. They're just basic black pants and a white top. If this is some sort of prank, it's the most epic one ever.

I press the heels of my hands to my eyes.

"Oh dear. I can call an ambulance if you think we need one," the older woman says to the blond lady.

"No. I'm fine." Crawling upright, I steady myself. My body feels weird. Rubbery, almost. My knees are weak. I don't know what just happened or where the creepy old lady went, but I do know that I have to get home. Fast.

~~~

I'm still panting by the time I reach my house. Who was the lady at the harbor? I don't know how it's possible, but she looked like the old woman I've been dreaming about for months. Maybe I'm more tired than I thought. I did accidentally hand Dad sugar instead of salt at the restaurant yesterday. Turns out sweet eggs get sent back to the kitchen pretty fast.

I drag my keys out of my backpack and start fumbling with the lock. A full fifteen minutes after I left the docks, and my hands are *still* shaking. When I finally get my front door open, a warm, sweet smell hits my nose. Cinnamon. Dad has been baking a lot lately, trying to perfect his new waffle recipe. The last batch I saw was supposed to be in the shape of coffins, but they looked more like lopsided squares. His customers won't care. He'll name them something clever like Wonder Who Died Waffles and people will line up for them.

Trudging into the living room, I kick my sneakers off and sigh as the ancient chandelier begins to flicker.

Right. On. Cue.

I know we're just renting this house for now, but still. It's so old that the owners should be paying *us* to live here! The walls are covered with yellowed peeling wallpaper, and every time I turn on the bathroom sink, the pipes in the walls sound like they're having a dance party. Then there's the electricity, which never seems to work right. Mom calls it charming, but it took me less than five minutes to figure out that's just code for crummy. If we're stuck here forever, I might not survive.

The lights flicker again, only this time they don't come back on right away. I groan and feel my way to the top of the stairwell. When we first arrived, Mom and Dad let me pick my bedroom first. I remember being excited when I saw the crow's nest for the first time because houses back in Chicago don't have them. Really, it's just a tiny room in the attic where the walls are mostly windows. I guess they call it a crow's nest because of how far you can see when you're in there—like an actual bird's nest in the top of a tree. One window looks out over the docks. One looks out over the ocean. One looks out over the town.

And the last window...that one looks toward the light-house. The lighthouse where Molly supposedly vanished. I've spent plenty of hours watching it and have seen a lot of things. Kids running around and scaring each other. Tour groups. I even saw the History channel filming there once. But the one thing I've never seen is the ghost of Sweet Molly.

Thank goodness, I think. Eastport's legends are dumb, but there's something about Molly that actually bugs me. Maybe it's the fact that she was so young. Or maybe it's that her story is so sad. I don't know.

Lifting my camera from around my neck, I set it on my desk. Then I pull all of the shades down and flip on the little LED lights I have strung around the ceiling of my room. Falling onto my bed, I try to forget the old woman from the harbor.

My eyes grow heavy as I focus on the sound of rain plinking off my window. If I wasn't so tired, I'd take some pictures of the water streaking down the glass. I bet it would look cool. I tell myself I'll do it another time. Right now, I just need just a few minutes of sleep.

FIVE

I wake up with a start. There was a sound. At least I thought there was. I sit up, dazed. How long was I asleep for? Ten minutes, an hour? The light filtering in through the cracks in my window blinds is muted. Covering my eyes, I lift one. The sun is over the water now. That means it's late afternoon. Ho-ly cow. I slept all day.

Snatching my phone up off the bed, I look through the missed calls and texts. Three texts from Emmie, two texts from Dad, one from Bri, and three calls from Mom. My phone rings in my hand, startling me. It's Mom again.

I answer it as fast as I can. "Hello?"

"Mallory! There you are! I was just putting on my raincoat to come check on you." Her voice is tense.

"I'm sorry. I fell asleep."

"For six hours?" she asks. "Wasn't your phone on?"

I turn my phone to the side, noticing that it isn't on silent. Dad always jokes that the song I use for my ringtone is so loud it's going to make him deaf someday. How did I sleep through that?

"Never mind. I wanted to make sure you're okay. Mrs. James stopped at the restaurant and said she saw you—"

"I know, I know," I interrupt. "I should have gone in and listened to her story about the shadow, but it smells so *bad* in that shop."

The line goes silent. When Mom finally speaks again, her words make less sense than the bacon-covered donuts Dad keeps trying to make.

"No, I was going to say that Mrs. James saw you at the harbor digging around in the sand and was worried about you. Said you didn't seem yourself."

Digging? I didn't see Mrs. James at the harbor, and I definitely didn't do any digging when I was there. I look down at my bed, suddenly realizing for the first time that my sheets are covered in something dark and grainy.

Sand.

It's everywhere. Under my fingernails, on my pillowcase, it's even caked into the soles of my sneakers. The sneakers I know I took off when I got home.

My heart beats faster. I jump up, fear pulsing through

me. Wet, sandy footprints cover my wood floor. It looks like someone ran in circles around my bed. A lot of the prints are smudged, but at least one is clear enough for me to examine. There's a small circle imprinted on one that looks like it has a seven inside it.

Yikes. That's my shoe size.

"Mallory?"

I hear Mom's voice, suddenly remembering she's on the phone. I lift it back to my ear and croak out a *yes*.

"What were you doing at the harbor? Did you drop something?" She pauses for a moment and then adds, "I hope it wasn't one of your grandmother's good earrings. I told her she shouldn't have given them to you until you were eighteen."

"I didn't drop an earring," I say, then instinctively reach up and check to make sure I'm not wrong. Both earrings are securely in my ears.

"Then what were you looking for?" she presses.

I don't know how to answer that. I've never sleepwalked before, but I can't think of any other explanation for this. I'm covered in sand and don't remember anything from the past six hours. If I tell Mom the truth, she'll be worried about me. Knowing her, I'll never get another day to myself again. I rub at the goose bumps springing up on my arms, a bad feeling growing deep inside me.

"I...um... I was looking for my house key." My stomach churns with the lie.

Mom sighs. "I know you love that key chain Jenna made you, but it's broken. Your key falls off all the time. Maybe time to replace it?"

"Maybe," I mutter. Jenna is my best friend back in Chicago. The key chain is a picture of Navy Pier where we hung out a lot. It's pretty, but the plastic is cracked so the ring part is duct-taped on. I keep saying I'll get a new one, but it feels wrong. Like giving up and accepting that Chicago isn't part of my life anymore. Jenna either.

I can't do it.

Picking at the sand that's buried under my fingernails, I take a deep breath. "I gotta go, Mom. I'm sorry I scared you."

"Me too," she huffs. "We'll be home later than usual tonight. Your father wants to make a batch of Chill Up Your Spine Chili for tomorrow's special."

"Okay. I'll answer my phone from now on. Promise."

"Please do. And if you see Mrs. James again, make sure she knows you're all right. She was pretty rattled."

That makes two of us. I end the call with shaking hands. Part of me wants to know exactly what happened to me today, but another part of me is afraid to find out. Did I really sleep-walk out of my house and down to the harbor? The idea is scary.

I go through the rest of my texts. The ones from Dad

were just him checking in and reminding me to lock the door when I get home. Emmie just wanted to know if I can sleep over tonight. Normally I'd totally want to, but now I'm not sure that's a good idea.

sorry was asleep, I text Emmie.

The little dots pulse, telling me she's typing back.

asleep? how?

dad gave me the day off. I click send then take a lap around my room, looking for anything unusual. Everything looks normal. My door is shut, the LED lights are still on, and all the shades are closed. The only thing that looks different is my camera. I could've sworn I set it on my desk when I came in. Now it's lying on the floor.

I *never* leave my camera on the floor. It's expensive, and I don't have the money to buy a new one if something happens to it. Lifting it up, I inspect the lens. No cracks.

My phone dings again. It's another text from Emmie. wow. That's a first. wanna hang out?

I think on this for a minute, deciding that I'm way too creeped out to be alone. I type back quickly. can you come here?

The little dots pulse, then stop. I stare at my phone, wondering what's taking her so long to respond. Emmie is the queen of fast texting. Her thumbs move so fast they're pretty much just a blur.

I'm still waiting for her to answer me when the doorbell rings.

I don't move. Instead I look out my window, wishing I could see the front porch. Instead all I see is the street and a little of the sidewalk.

The doorbell rings again.

My hands go clammy. I wipe them off on my jeans and laugh. I'm being ridiculous. Just because I had a strange afternoon doesn't mean there's something bad on my doorstep right now. *Unless there is.* The old woman from the harbor pops into my head. I shake off the thought and walk over to my door, pausing with my hand on the doorknob.

The text alert on my phone goes off, making me jump.

you gonna let me in or what?

I let the breath out I was holding. Emmie has been the one ringing my doorbell. Not the creepy woman from the harbor. Not a murderous clown. Not...well, whatever. Just Emmie.

coming, I type back.

I take the stairs two at a time until I hit the first floor. The chandelier flickers. Ignoring it, I skid to a stop in front of the front door. Emmie rushes in, her pale cheeks flushed with cold.

"Sheesh! What took you so long?" She shrugs out of her jacket and flops down on the couch. As usual, she's in a sweatshirt and jeans. Her auburn curls are loose today, draping down over her shoulders and making her green eyes look even greener. I shove my own hair out of my eyes, wishing once again I had just one feature of Emmie's. My hair is brown. My eyes are brown. I'm...what would you call it? *Unremarkable.*

I drop down beside her. "I'm sorry. This hasn't been the best day."

Her eyebrows knit together. "Wait, really? I was just joking. What happened?"

The better question is, what *didn't* happen.

When I don't answer right away, she looks from me to the door and then back again. "Does this have anything to do with the sand all over the floor? Your mom is gonna kill you if that isn't swept up by the time she gets home."

I follow her line of sight to the door. My breath hitches. I hadn't noticed it before, but the floor is covered with sand and footprints. My footprints. These are clearer than the ones up in my room, so clear that I can see the logo from my shoes perfectly.

SIX

I sink down onto the couch, feeling overwhelmed. If there was any doubt that I was sleepwalking, it's gone now.

"Mal?" Emmie lays a hand on my shoulder, shaking me gently. "What's going on? You're so pale."

"I'm always pale," I mumble.

She snorts. "True, but not like this."

I can feel Emmie watching me, so I angle myself toward her. "Dad gave me the day off because I haven't been sleeping well."

"The dreams," she says. Emmie knows all about my nightmares. She's the only one who does. I've thought about telling Brianne, but she's not like Emmie and me. She's into acting and goes to Harbor Point so she can become a famous actress someday. That means she can be a little dramatic, and if there's one thing I don't need more of right now, it's drama.

I nod. "But on my way home, there was this woman at the harbor."

Letting my eyes drift shut for a moment, I try to remember her. I'm sure I imagined it, but she really did remind me of the old woman from my dreams.

"Anyway," I continue. "Something happened."

"Something bad?"

"Yeah. There was a storm, and the woman's eyes were all wild looking, and she kept asking me, *Where is it?*, and—"

Emmie hold a hand up, looking lost. "Wait. Where is *what*?"

"That's just it! I don't know. The whole thing was scary, so I came home and went to sleep." My gaze travels back to the sand on the floor. "At least I thought I did. I woke up six hours later to a house with more sand in it than the beach. Also, Mrs. James said she saw me at the harbor. *Digging.*"

Emmie's eyes are wide, her mouth hanging open in an *O* shape.

"So, all this sand. You really don't remember how it got here?" she asks quietly, tucking herself deeper into the couch cushions.

"I don't remember anything, Em. The last thing I remember I was lying in bed, listening to the sound of the rain on my windows."

After a long pause, Emmie pulls on a familiar smile. It's

the same one she uses when she's working at her mom's candy shop. She's worked part-time at Spirits and Sweets since we were ten and has perfected the *I'm-sick-of tourists-but-can't-act-like-it* smile.

"There's a rational explanation for this," she finally says.

I can't help but smirk. "You mean, there's a *curse* for this. Maybe I forgot to hold my breath when I passed one of the graveyards this week. This"—I wave my hand around at the sand scattered across the floor—"is probably just the beginning. Next you know, I'll be haunted or possessed or something."

"Pfft, *right*." She rolls her eyes as she draws out the word. "You don't believe in any of that stuff. And you know I don't either. I mean, if any of the curse nonsense around here was real, I should've died seven or eight times by now."

With this, she starts laughing. It's loud, a deep belly laugh that always gets me going too. Before I know it, I'm clutching my aching stomach and swiping at the tears building in my eyes. This is exactly why we became friends. While everyone else in Eastport is celebrating these stupid curses, Emmie is trying to disprove them. It makes her cool in my opinion. Unfortunately, it also makes her a teeny-tiny bit unpopular around here.

The problem is that most everybody in this town loves

the curses. They love the attention and the tourists those stories bring to Eastport. Not me and Emmie, though.

"Look," she slaps my leg playfully. "Whatever happened today, we'll figure it out. You've got me on the case now."

It's a pretty comforting thought, to be honest. Emmie isn't a detective, but she might as well be. She's *that* good at figuring things out. Five months ago, she set out to find out if Edward Gaunt—the man Gaunt Street is named after—actually fell into wet concrete and got buried into the foundation of the famous Eastport Inn. Sounds bananas, but people come from all over the country to stay at the inn because of that! It took her forever, but Emmie dug up enough documentation to prove that Mr. Gaunt died of old age. Just boring old oldness. When she showed the owners of the inn her evidence, they called her parents.

It was *not* a happy call.

Her parents insisted she burn her evidence and never talk about Mr. Gaunt or the Eastport Inn ever again. They also took her phone for a month. A month! Ever since then, Emmie has kept her theories to herself. I would too. Telling the truth around here is like smashing a beehive. There might be a sweet reward, but you're definitely gonna get stung.

"Or maybe we don't even have a case," I suggest hopefully. "I mean, maybe today was just weird, but now it's over."

Emmie looks skeptical. She walks over to the nearest shoe print in the sand and snaps a picture of it with her cell phone. "Maybe. But you've been having nightmares on and off since you moved here. The sleepwalking could have something to do with that."

I look up, feeling like she read my mind. "I was wondering that too. I'm so tired all the time. I read once that being overtired can make sleepwalking worse."

"Makes sense." Her head bobs up and down. "The only problem is you've never sleepwalked before, and today isn't the first day you've been tired."

Lightning suddenly flashes outside. The wind picks up, thrashing rain against the front windows. I bet Mom and Dad are thrilled. Bad storms make Mom's dramatizations more popular than ever. She probably has the customers halfway to a heart attack by now.

I watch the droplets of rain streak down the front window, considering the thought that has been bothering me for a while. "The woman from the harbor this afternoon... She looked a little like the old woman from my nightmares."

Emmie goes still. "Why didn't you tell me that right away?"

My hands twist together painfully in my lap. "Because it makes no sense. The woman in my dreams isn't real. This woman was. I mean, I think she was. I don't know."

Emmie stands up abruptly. The chandelier flickers.

"Where are you going?" I ask.

"To get a broom to clean up this mess. I really don't know what happened to you today, but we need to figure it out. And we won't be able to do that if your mother kills you first."

"And how exactly are you going to do that?"

"You mean *we*," she says, snatching a broom out of the coat closet. "There's only one way to find out if the woman you saw today was real or not. We're going back to the harbor to see if she's still there."

SEVEN

A streak lights up the gray sky, followed by a menacing rumble of thunder. I huddle against Emmie, wishing we had more than one umbrella. Eastport is pretty in the summer—filled with turquoise water and flowers. But in October, every day doesn't just look like Halloween; it feels like it too.

"Think we should call Bri?" Emmie poses, leaping over a large puddle in her path.

"So, she can freak out about this?" I laugh. "I'm thinking no. I love her and all, but something tells me she wouldn't make this easier exactly."

Emmie breaks into a howl of laughter.

"What?" I ask.

She waits until she can catch her breath, wiping a stray tear from her eye. "I was just imagining her using what happened to you as her next monologue at school. You'd be famous around Eastport within hours!"

Well that settles it. *Definitely* not calling Brianne.

The harbor comes into view. I pause. The last time I was here—well, the last time I *remember* being here—was one of the scariest experiences of my life. I understand why Emmie suggested we come back here, but now that we're here I really want to go home.

"You were standing where, exactly?" Emmie asks, tugging me along. The lights strung from the roof of the bait shop are lit up now—little bats and pumpkins gleaming in the drizzle.

I point to the edge of the dock where I'd first seen the Mrs. Barry lookalike. "Right there."

I replay the whole scene in my mind. I'd put my hand on the woman's shoulder to get her attention. She'd turned around. *Skin stretched thin over bones. White eyes. Rags for clothes.* Everything I can remember matches the woman who shows up in my dreams at night. The only difference is, this woman said something.

Emmie has given up on staying dry under our little umbrella and is pacing the dock. "Were there any other people here when this happened? Another witness?"

Her question jogs a memory. "Yes! There was a woman with a stroller. She stopped to see if I was okay."

"Did you recognize her?" Her face lights up with the idea. "Maybe we could find her and ask what she saw."

I shake my head. "No. I was kind of out of it, but I didn't recognize her."

"Bummer," Emmie responds, her mouth tilting downward. Rain is dripping from her hair now, making her curls more defined. "Well, there's no one here now."

I turn a full circle, searching for anyone...*anything* that could help us figure out what happened to me today. My eyes land on a patch of sand just off the dock. It looks disturbed, churned up like a little kid was digging to make a sandcastle or moat. Could that be from me?

Walking over, I hop down off the dock and immediately gasp. I was wrong. There isn't just one spot where the sand is torn up. There are *dozens*.

"Whoa," Emmie breathes out as she pulls up to my side. "Do you think you did this?"

"I guess I had to, right?" I scan the area, noticing that the holes are all different sizes, shapes, and depths. If I didn't know better, I'd think a dog did this. It looks *that* manic.

We both kneel down and inspect the holes. Rain is starting to pool in them, creating miniature tide pools. I grab a stick and start sticking it down into the holes one at a time. They're deeper than I expected them to be.

"What were you looking for Mal?"

Something worth digging a zillion holes for, I guess. Must be important. Apparently not important enough to remember, though.

I sit back on my heels, confused. This had to have taken me a long time. How is it that I don't remember any of it?

"This is so annoying. I can't shake the feeling that these things are connected. The holes and the woman from the harbor," I pose.

"Connected how? From what it sounds like, you ran into a weird old woman who creeped you out. You went home, fell asleep, and sleepwalked." She shrugs. "I don't see a connection there."

"Think about it," I start. "The old woman kept asking, *Where is it?* That sounds like she was looking for something. It seems coincidental that I would then sleepwalk back here and start digging holes like *I'm* looking for something."

Emmie reaches over and presses a cold, wet palm to my forehead.

"What are you doing?" I ask, swatting her away.

"Checking to see if you have a fever since you're obviously delirious," she cackles.

I fold my arms over my chest, annoyed. "Emmilene Harris!"

She frowns at my use of her full name—a full name she hates more than almonds in chocolate. "Seriously?"

"You gave me no choice. I'm being serious here. I think there's something we're missing, and you're making fun of me."

"Okay, okay," Emmie says, "I'm sorry. This whole thing just seems, I don't know, unlike you?"

"I know. I don't know how else to explain it. It's kind of like a gut feeling." A gut feeling that something is wrong. Very, very wrong. "I need to find that woman. She targeted me for a reason, and I want to know what it is."

Emmie's eyes darken. "All right. But if you actually think these holes are somehow connected to the woman who freaked you out, then we have a bigger problem than I thought."

"Why?"

"Because that would mean what happened today was paranormal. Like, the kind of thing everyone in this town *hopes* will happen to them."

"There's no such thing as ghosts. Or curses. Or...whatever that old woman wants me to think she is! It's probably just some random lady who wants to be the newest legend around here." I scrub my hands down my face, frustrated. I didn't think it was possible to be more confused than I am, but I guess I was wrong.

"Did you hear me?" Emmie asks.

"I'm sorry. I was spaced out. What?"

Emmie gives me a look, then stands up. Her knees are covered with wet sand. "I said my mom just texted. I gotta get home to babysit Goober."

Goober isn't her brother's actual name, of course, but Emmie thinks it fits him better than his real name, which is Steven. I can't say she's wrong. Steven is a round toddler with red cheeks and perpetually sticky fingers. He communicates through grunts and screams. All in all, he's not that fun to be around. Definitely a Goober.

I stand up and hand her the umbrella, but she pushes it away. "Do I look like that thing can help me now?" she laughs. "My hair is going to be a frizzy mess no matter what. Plus, you have a longer walk home than me."

"See you tomorrow?" I ask, giving her a quick hug.

"Totally. I have to work for a little while and don't forget we're on picture duty. But we can talk more then."

Ugh. Picture duty. I forgot about that. Every month, our school chooses three students to take photos of the parade to go in the local newspaper—the *Eastport Eerie*. This time, my name was pulled. So was Emmie's. I don't know who the third person is. Guess we'll find out when we get there.

Blowing me a kiss, Emmie skips off in the rain like she doesn't have a care in the world. I wish I didn't. Instead, my brain feels heavy. I head back toward home, dodging puddles since I didn't take the time to change out of my new shoes. Blah. I can feel my feet squishing around in them which means it's too late. They'll never look new again.

I'm standing on my front porch, dripping wet and digging through my pockets for my keys when I catch a glimpse of someone looking out the window next door. The white-blond hair gives it away. *Joshua.* Joshua Bergen has lived next door as long as I've been in Eastport, and I'm pretty sure in all that time, he's said seven words to me. He goes to Harbor Point too, but I heard he's into painting, not photography. That would explain why we've only been in one class together. He's a quiet guy who reminds me a little bit of the crabs that run up and down the shoreline in the summer. At the first hint of a person, they run into a hole and hide.

I lift a pruny hand to wave at him, but the curtains snap shut. Jamming my key into the lock, I open the door and start kicking the sand off my shoes before I step in. I take one look back at Josh's window, startling when I notice that although the curtains are still shut, they're sheer enough for me to see Josh is still standing behind them.

Still watching me.

EIGHT

I've just gotten into dry clothes and eaten some leftover rice from the fridge when Mom and Dad get home. As usual, they're loud. Some kids complain because their parents fight all the time, but mine are different. They make each other laugh. A *lot*.

"Hey, sweetie!" Dad crows. He strips off his jacket and hangs it on the back of the kitchen chair. As usual, his shirt is speckled with something. Ghoulish Gravy, maybe? "We got you something on the way home."

He digs into his jeans pocket and pulls out something shiny. A key ring. I turn it over in my hand, trying not to show how disappointed I am. It's silver and features a silhouette Sweet Molly. Underneath, the words *The Girl in White* are etched into the metal.

"Thanks," I mutter, silently vowing never to use it. I understand that we live in Eastport and that there's no hope of moving back home anytime soon but giving up my old key ring and using this one makes it seem like I'm okay with that.

Mom sets a paper bag on the kitchen counter. I peek over the top of it, spotting take-out containers. "What did you bring back? Any dessert?"

She smirks. "Would we ever come home without dessert for you?"

I dig into the cartons, smiling when I find what I'm looking for. A tub of homemade chocolate pudding. Leftover rice isn't that satisfying. But chocolate...now that's a different story, and Dad's recipe is awesome. The way he tells it, his great-great-grandmother used to make it all the time. Like a lot of the food he cooks, the recipe got handed down from generation to generation until it because his trademark dessert at The Hill—Put It in Formaldehyde Pudding. I take the first bite, groaning as the perfect combo of chocolate and whipped cream hits my taste buds.

"I presume that sound means you approve?" he asks with a conspiratorial grin.

"Absolutely," I say around a mouthful of pudding. I drop my spoon back into the container, my good mood quickly souring as I remember that this pudding is just a distraction.

I have problems—serious problems—waiting for me. "Can I take this up to my room? I have picture duty tomorrow and need to make sure my camera and memory cards are all set up."

Mom eyes the container and chuckles. "Sure thing. But don't make yourself sick. That's a lot of sugar."

Good. I need a lot of sugar. Even when I thought I had a full day to rest, I ended up sleepwalking and I still feel tired.

"Oh, by the way—I'll be at the parade tomorrow too," Dad says.

I hover by the kitchen door, cradling my pudding. "Why?"

Since the parade happens every month, it's pretty short. Beginning to end, I think it's about thirty minutes. I get that the mayor thinks it's good for Eastport tourism, but if you ask me, it's just a giant hassle. Plus, it's boring. I can't imagine why Dad wants to go.

"I guess the city council decided to add food booths to it for this month," he answers. "You know, a little something extra since it is our busiest month of the year. The Hill will have one there on Sunday and then a much larger one at the anniversary festival."

"How is that going to work with Mom at the restaurant and you at the parade?"

"Dad will only be at the parade long enough to help set up. He's leaving Janine at the booth, and the chili is already premade," Mom clarifies. "I'll be at the restaurant with Arthur. He can handle the cooking while Dad is out."

"So, you won't need me?"

Dad shakes his head. "I don't think so, kiddo. Not with the parade. It will probably be less busy in the restaurant, so you do what you need to do for school."

"Got it." I turn on my heel and head upstairs, realizing halfway up that the pudding tub had some chocolate around the rim that is now around my sweatshirt. Oh, well. Seems pretty on-brand for today.

My bedroom is dim with just the LED lights on. I turn on a lamp and set the pudding on my desk. Then I turn my attention to the camera. While some kids might get excited about new clothes or bikes or skincare products, I get excited about my camera. I got it as a gift from my grandparents when I got into Harbor Point. Since then, it has been at my side about as much as Emmie has.

Turning it on, I decide to scan my most recent shots first. They should be of the fog from a few days ago. It was creeping through the streets of Eastport like little tendrils of smoke. The day was gloomy too, so the end result was a picture that looked like it had a black-and-white filter on it but didn't.

When the viewing screen turns on, I freeze. The last picture taken isn't one I recognize. Instead of the fog, it's of the harbor. The harbor I was just at with Emmie.

I narrow my eyes on the image. It's blurry and out of focus. Did I take this while I was sleepwalking?

Turning the brightness up on my screen, I examine it closely. Even though it isn't focused properly, I can see the outline of the holes in the sand. They're not as random looking as they were when I saw them in person. They're in a pattern...a shape. I squint harder, sucking in a shocked breath when I realize they form letters.

S...T...O...P.

Stop. The holes in the sand spell out the word *stop*.

NINE

I set the camera down with shaking hands. *Stop*. Stop what? And why would I dig that word into the sand?

My stomach does a flip-flop. Suddenly my pudding doesn't seem that great. I walk in tight circles around my small room, desperate to put all the pieces of this messed up puzzle together.

I'm just about to text Emmie when I hear a loud squeak in my closet.

I go stone still, my heart thumping in my chest so hard it feels like it could burst out. There's a trickling sound now. Like water, only not quite.

Another squeak, this one longer and drawn out like someone is slowly stepping on an old floorboard.

"Hello?" My voice comes out shaky. "Is someone there?"

Silence.

I take a step toward the closet. My legs feel weak and rubbery.

The trickling slows until I can't hear it anymore. All I hear now is my own heartbeat echoing in my ears. I take another step. A loud bang stops me in my tracks. That's it. There's definitely something in my closet.

A flash of lightning brightens my room, followed by a crash of thunder in the distance. *Great.* The storm is back. Right in time to help this house give me a heart attack.

Taking a few quick steps, I try to shake off the awful ideas rumbling around in my head. Something is behind my closet door. Maybe something as simple as a cat, but how would it have gotten in there? There are no windows in my closet. No ways for a random animal to get in.

This house *is* wacky though. There are bathrooms so small you can hardly turn around in them, and everything— and I mean *everything*—is creaky. Maybe there's a hole or a vent in my closet I never noticed?

The thunder gets louder and the feeling starts up. It's the one I get all the time here, like I'm being watched. But how is it possible that someone could be watching me in my own bedroom? I swivel around to make sure the shades are still closed. They are. I glance at my laptop, lying open on my desk.

The little camera cover is slid shut too. There's no one here. No one except me and whatever is in my closet.

With a few final steps, I close the gap between me and the closet and lay a shaky hand on the doorknob. It's now or never.

Flinging the door open, I squeeze my eyes shut out of instinct. Slowly, I open one and then the other. There isn't a cat in my closet. There's water. My mouth drops open as I stare at the floor. A thin layer of liquid ripples across the wood, like something leaked.

I immediately look up to the ceiling and across the walls. There are no cracks, no holes…nothing that could be leaking. Running my hand across the walls, I shake my head in confusion. They're dry. Kneeling down, I cautiously touch a finger to the water. It's cold as ice.

A sharp crack of thunder rattles my windowpanes. I scream, then quickly clap a hand over my mouth. The room lights up with another wild zigzag of lightning. I scoot away from the closet. Under any other circumstances, a little water wouldn't be scary. But after a day like today, it's terrifying.

My bedroom door bursts open. Mom and Dad rush in, their eyes wild.

"Mallory!" Dad says. "What happened? Are you okay?"

I look from them to the closet. How do I answer that? I want to tell them everything. The dreams. The sleepwalking.

The woman at the harbor and the holes in the sand. Maybe they'd be able to help. Or *maybe* they'd do what parents do sometimes and suggest something totally unhelpful. Last month Bri was upset because this guy at school—a guy she crushes on big-time—never likes any of her posts even though she likes all his. Her parents kept asking her what was wrong. Bri finally told them, and they didn't get it. At all. Rather than just listening, they ended up taking her cell phone for a week so she could get offline and enjoy the real world a bit.

Ugh.

"I'm sorry," I start. My voice trembles. "The thunder just scared me is all."

Please don't let them look in my closet. Please, please.

Mom lifts a hand to her chest and laughs. "And here I thought I was the queen of scares."

Laughing awkwardly, I nudge the closet door shut then quickly sit on my bed to draw their attention away from it. My entire body is still shaking. I pull the quilt from the end of my bed and wrap it around myself, hoping my parents think I'm just chilled.

"You're sure you're okay?" Dad presses, his forehead bunched up into worried lines.

Pffft. Not. Even. Close.

"I'm good. Promise." I make a show of stretching. "I think I just need to go to sleep. Big day tomorrow."

Mom's face lights up. "I'm so glad you're finally getting into the local traditions here. The parade can be fun, Mal. Especially when you have a job like you do tomorrow."

I nod, even though I don't agree. The parade sounds like anything but fun. Every time I hear the off-key droning of the bone piano, I get uncomfortable. It's stupid, I know. I can't help it, though. Something about that whole parade just feels...off.

"Right. I'll get some good shots for sure," I mumble. Still, my mind is stuck on the water in my closet and the word spelled out in the sand.

Dad crosses to my bed and plants a kiss on the top of my head. "Get some sleep."

I don't answer. Instead, I burrow down underneath my covers. I don't even care that I'm still in jeans. I'm tired and worried. But more than that, I'm confused. My brain is still telling me there's an explanation for all of this. I just wish I knew how to find it.

My parents walk out, leaving my door open just a crack. Good. Before we moved here, I might've gotten up and shut it. Privacy and all. But not tonight. Tonight, I don't want to feel alone.

I want to feel safe.

TEN

She's beckoning to me. A tattered white dress clings to her mottled skin, occasionally billowing out in the breeze. I stare open-mouthed at the old woman. Her skeletal finger is crooked, urging me forward. When she realizes I'm not coming to her, her eyes darken.

Turning to run away, I realize I'm at the bottom of the rocks by the lighthouse. I try to climb up them, but they tear at my palms and bare feet. I can't move. I can hardly breathe. All that's left is the sensation that I'm doomed.

That we're all doomed.

~~~~~

When the alarm goes off, my eyes are already open. I dreamed about her again. *All night.* I sit up, every muscle in my body screaming even though I didn't work out yesterday. Unless you count walking up the stairs to my bedroom being exercise. I lift both arms over my head and stretch out, wincing at the pain.

Did she cause this? The thought pops into my head so quickly I don't have time to think about how dumb it is. The woman from my dreams is just my imagination getting the better of me. Like movies. I don't watch a lot of horror films, but Emmie does. She loves the jump scares. Not me. I see one and have dreams for days. All the stupid legend talk around Eastport is probably the same. It wormed its way into my brain and is making me dream things. See things.

Goose bumps rise on my arms as I look toward my closet. The door is still partially open. I shove my blankets off, telling myself to stop being a chicken. All this time in Eastport and I've never bought into any of the stupid scary stories. Why should I now?

I open the closet door slowly, surprised to see that the floor is dry. There are no water marks and no damp areas either. Maybe Mom snuck back in here after I was asleep and cleaned it up? No. She didn't know the water was there to begin with, so that couldn't be.

Digging around in the piles of clothes lying around my room, I come up with a mostly clean sweatshirt and jeans. I tug them on, then search for my hat. Most stuff I brought from Chicago is no good here. Like my bike. I imagined taking long rides along the ocean but realized pretty quick that the streets here are too narrow, too busy, and too hilly for that. They're also cobblestone, which means they're super bumpy and more than a little dangerous. Riding a bike on them is only a good idea if you're comfortable taking a trip over your handlebars at least once a week.

The knit cap, though? It's still a winner. Eastport is warm in the summertime, but this time of year, the breeze coming in off the ocean is chilly. I pull it down over my messy hair, grateful that if I have to be a part of this creepy little parade today, at least I'll have warm ears.

The distant ring of the doorbell pulls my attention away. Gentle thuds move from one end of the house to the other, probably one of my parents answering the door.

"Mallory?" Dad's voice echoes up the stairs. "Emmie is here."

"Coming!" I grab my camera off the desk and loop the strap around my neck then head down.

Emmie is sitting cross-legged on the couch when I get there. She's got a thick knit sweater on with a matching white stocking cap. It makes her hair and eyes even brighter. She unzips her coat a little further and gives me a tight smile.

"You good today?" She asks, raising an eyebrow. "Bri texted me like three times last night asking about you. She said you didn't answer her texts?"

I open my mouth to answer her, but Dad walks in, holding a plate.

"These are the sides for the chili today. Thought you ladies might like one with some honey."

"Biscuits?" I ask.

"You got it!" He sets the plate down on the table along with two napkins. "Boneyard biscuits, made fresh this morning."

Unlike a normal-shaped biscuit, Dad's are shaped like tombstones. The steam rising from them reminds me of Eastport's cemeteries on foggy mornings.

"Yes," Emmie says, drawing out the word as she snags a biscuit, then tosses it back and forth between her hands. "Ooh. Hot, hot, hot!"

I laugh. "Easy, tiger. I've never seen the ER here, but I bet it isn't all that fun."

Emmie ignores me and takes a massive first bite. "Totally worth it."

I laugh at the crumbs sticking to her ChapStick-covered lips. I joke all the time that Emmie has a bottomless stomach, but it's totally true. Pretty sure she could win one of those hot dog eating challenges I see on television every Fourth of July.

Emmie dips her biscuit into the honey again and takes a second bite. "So good, Mr. Denton. And so unfair."

"Oh yeah? How's that?" Dad asks.

"You make your daughter fresh biscuits for breakfast. My mom offered me last night's leftover taco meat." She wrinkles up her nose. "It was gross the first time around!"

Dad laughs loudly. "Well, I'm glad you approve! Let's hope my customers do too!"

"They will," I add. I might not love The Hill, but I love how proud he is of it. Both my parents are. Becoming an adult sounds awful, but since I know it's going to happen no matter what I do, I hope I end up like them. Happy and doing something I love. Hopefully that something is taking pictures.

"Okay, Mom is already at the restaurant and I'm headed down to Gaunt Street to make sure everything is all set up for Janette. You guys can get where you need to be on your own?"

I snort. Back in Chicago, that was a thing. If I needed to be somewhere, odds were good one of my parents would have to drive me. It's a huge city. Here, though? There are not that many streets, and I'm pretty sure no one here has experienced a traffic jam. Unless Emmie and I get lost during one of our cemetery shortcuts, I don't see how it would be possible for us *not* to get where we need to be.

"Yeah, we're good. Thanks." I give Dad a hug and wrap the other biscuit up in a napkin to take with me even though I'm not hungry. Today could be long, and I don't think we'll have time for lunch. "Wanna finish on the way?"

A muffled yes comes from Emmie. She wipes her mouth with one of the napkins, but not before I can catch a glimpse of the crumbs dotting her chin. They look like a crumb-beard. I laugh thinking that it sounds like another legend around here—the curse of Crumb-Beard.

Emmie and I wind through two real graveyards and several fake ones on our way down to the parade route. The morning sun is warm despite the chill in the air, and I feel my spirits lifting with each step. Dad always used to say *tomorrow is a new day*. I didn't really get what that means until now. But today really is a new day. All the horrible stuff from last night feels fuzzy...distant. Like my dry closet floor, I'm already beginning to feel normal again.

Thank goodness.

"So. Anything else happen last night after I went home?" Her question puts a crack in the little bit of peace I found. I don't want it to shatter entirely, so I lie.

"No. Not really." Guilt churns in my stomach. I shouldn't be lying to Emmie. I already lied to my parents! But I feel good right now. Better than I have in a while. Talking about yesterday feels dangerous, like it will mess everything up.

She grins. "Good! Because that was a little much, even for me. Still, we have a lot of figuring out to do."

I wave off the idea like it's silly. "I was probably just overtired, Em. It all seems kinda stupid now, doesn't it?"

She narrows her eyes skeptically. "I don't know. Does it? You were pretty scared yesterday. And those holes down by the harbor looked pretty real."

So did the word *stop* spelled out in the sand. And the water in my closet. And the...well, everything. But that was all yesterday. Yesterday sucked. Today is a new day, and it's going to be better.

Right?

ELEVEN

We reach the registration desk right on time. Even though the parade doesn't officially start until noon, they like everyone checked in early in case someone doesn't show up and they need to call for a backup.

"I gotta run to the bathroom," Emmie whispers. "Can you check us both in?"

"No problem. Just meet me back here."

I turn back to the check-in desk. It's decked out with a black-and-white tablecloth and big jack-o'-lantern center-pieces. An older woman with cobwebs painted across her pale cheeks asks for my name, then crosses it off from a list on her clipboard. "You on photography duty?"

"Yup," I say, lifting my camera to show her.

"Excellent. There are a few surprises lined up today,

so be on your toes!" She grins, and the cobweb on her cheek shifts. The little spider disappears with her wrinkles, making the whole thing look more like a lopsided fishing net.

I give her Emmie's name too, and she hands me two wads of bright orange fabric.

"Oh, uh...what are these?" I ask.

"They're your anniversary sweatshirts, dear!" she chirps. The witch's hat perched on top of her graying hair bobs around. "One for each of you. Everyone who works at an event this month will get one. Wear it as often as you can. Good for business," she says with a wink.

Good for business, bad for fashion. I hold the shirt up, frowning at the image printed on the front. It's the lighthouse with a boat in the distance. The *Merriweather*. That's the boat that Sweet Molly's brother, Liam was the captain of. There's lightning in the sky above the boat and the waves around it are big. A small figure stands on top of the rocks around the lighthouse. It's supposed to be Sweet Molly herself. I'm sure of it.

"Creepy, huh?" A voice pipes up behind me.

I turn around, shocked to see *him*. Joshua Bergen, a.k.a the weird kid next door who was watching me yesterday. What's he doing here?

"Yeah," I answer, looking down to avoid his eyes. Little does he know the creepiest thing here is him. "Creepy."

Keeping my gaze firmly rooted to the ground, I notice his shoes. Custom high-top Converse. They're black with orangish-red cliffs and mountains on them. There's a sun too. It looks like a desert scene.

"Like them?" He asks, doing a little dance with his feet.

I finally look up and meet his eyes. They're very blue, twinkling in the sunlight. His mouth is quirked up at the edges, his blond hair swept across his forehead at an angle.

"They're cool," I admit, looking back down. "They remind me of the Sahara or something."

"Not quite," he answers. "That's in Africa. This is the Sonoran. It's in Arizona."

Interesting. Most custom Converse I've seen have things on them like movie characters, quotes, or song lyrics. This is my first time seeing a desert.

"You like deserts?"

He laughs. "I guess? I mean, I used to live in the Sonoran. Before I moved here a few years ago."

The tone of his voice is familiar. He doesn't sound happy about having moved to Eastport. He sounds sad, like he misses the Sonoran Desert. Like me with Chicago.

"What's the writing at the bottom?" I ask, deciding to change the topic. If he feels even half as sad about moving as I still do, he probably doesn't want to talk about it.

He tilts his shoe to the side so I can see it more clearly. In small white letters near the bottom are the words *acta, non verba*. "It's Latin."

"Oh." It's really all I can think to say. I don't know much about Latin, but it seems like an odd thing to have added to a perfectly good pair of custom shoes.

"Anyway, I bet they made you come to this today to take pictures, huh?" He gestures at my camera.

"Yeah. Me and Emmie both." I notice Joshua is wearing a backpack splattered with bits of multicolored paint. "Did they make you come here to paint something?"

Photographs, I can understand. But paintings? That's weird. I've never seen Joshua paint, but my other friends who do need stuff like a canvas and easel and a lot of different materials. I look around the street, noting how busy it is. Vendors and volunteers are everywhere, hanging balloons, handing out shirts, and setting up stands. Doesn't seem like an ideal place to try to paint something.

Joshua shrugs. "Sorta. I'm supposed to 'attend the parade and see what inspires me,' then go from there." He laughs. "Right now, I'm not inspired by anything but the smell coming from your dad's stand."

I turn to face the row of tents across the street. Three tents down is a black one adorned with plastic skeletons and coffins hanging from the front. Janette is inside, straining to stir something inside an oversized black cauldron.

Yup. That would belong to The Hill all right.

I sigh. "That smell is today's special. Chill Up Your Spine Chili."

He clutches his stomach and groans. "Should've eaten at home this morning, because according to this"—he waves a piece of paper out in the air between us—"there are no breaks until the parade is over."

Reaching a hand into my pocket, I pull out the napkin-wrapped biscuit I never ate. "Still warm, if you want it."

His eyes light up. "What kind of a maniac doesn't want a warm biscuit?"

"The kind that's sick of her parents' creepy restaurant?" I ask, but it isn't a question. It's the truth.

"Joshua Bergen," a female voice pipes up over the speakers. A horrible squall of feedback follows, prompting everyone to cover their ears. "Please report to the town square."

I slowly uncover my ears and Joshua does the same.

Joshua clears his throat. "That was extreme. Guess I should go." He lifts the biscuit in the air. "Thanks for this."

He turns to walk away, but I can't let that happen. Not until I understand why he was watching me yesterday and why he didn't want me to see him.

"Wait!"

He stops and turns around.

Just do it, Mallory. I steel myself to ask the question.

"Why were you watching me yesterday?" I swallow hard, nerves taking over. "When I got home, I saw you. In your window."

Joshua stares at me for a long minute. Too long. Finally, he leans in like he's going to share a secret with me. "I know what happened yesterday. I was watching you because it happened to me too."

The wind is knocked out of me. "H-how?"

"Not here," he whispers, his eyes darting around. "After the parade. My house. We can talk about it then."

He says it so confidently that I nod without thinking.

He tips his head like we're in agreement, then walks away. Emmie is at my side in an instant.

"What was that? Was that Joshua Bergen? What was he saying to you?" Her questions tumble out so fast I hold a hand up to stop her.

"*Shhhh.* Yes, it was Joshua. I'm meeting him after the parade. He has something to tell me. Something about what happened yesterday."

Emmie looks like she's been slapped. "Are you serious, Mal? No. No way. If you're meeting him, I am too. We don't know him at all. He could be a murderer!"

He didn't seem like a murderer. He didn't even seem that weird or shy. He seemed...nice?

"Relax. I don't think he's a murderer. A little wacky, maybe." I look back in the direction we walked off in just to make sure he can't overhear. "I know you like to know everything about people and all, but there might not be time to, you know, investigate Joshua right now. If he can help make sense of what happened? I need to talk to him. Soon."

She shakes her head, sending her red curls out and into the breeze. "I thought you were just *overtired*. You told me the whole thing seemed stupid now."

She feels left out, like I chose to talk to a total stranger about this over her. I reach out and squeeze her hand, hoping she understands that's not what happened.

"I was just saying that to make myself feel better. But something else *did* happen last night after you left and I can't... I can't just forget about it." The picture still sitting on my camera pops into my mind. The holes and the word *stop*. I should've shown Emmie right away this morning. If she feels left out now, she's going to be downright angry with me when I tell her about that later.

Hurt flashes behind Emmie's eyes. "But you said—"

"Please spread out, girls," a burly man wearing an orange anniversary shirt and a face full of white makeup says, interrupting us. "The event organizers would like pictures of everything, including setup." He grins, the black paint on his lips cracking to reveal thin, white lines. "Can't very well do that if you're bunched up here, eh?"

Emmie and I break apart, but not before she shoots me a look. A look that says I better be ready to explain myself later. But for now, I have a parade I want no part of beginning to take shape in front of me. Oh, and those surprises that check-in lady told me to keep an eye out for.

TWELVE

I wander the parade route, snapping pictures of anything even a little bit interesting. A face painter setting up her palette and brushes. An organizer barking out orders to the men moving the bone key piano. A child peering out of a window, waiting for the festivities to start.

Then I see Molly. Well, the girl they've chosen to play her for this parade, anyway. It's Sarah McHalloran, an eighth grader at Harbor Point. I look her up and down, taking in the flowing white gown and delicate slippers on her feet. Sarah's blond hair is styled into two messy braids that drape over her shoulders, just like every image of Sweet Molly I've ever seen, and her lips are painted a very pale pink. She wouldn't look half bad if it weren't for the dark streaks of mascara smeared down her porcelain cheeks, giving her a tormented, just-crawled-out-of-the-grave vibe.

"Mallory!" she shrieks, giving a twirl so her gown billows out around her. "Can you believe this? It's awesome, right?"

"Awesome," I repeat, feeling unsettled. "You look just like her."

"Thanks," she responds, grinning. "And once I get into character, it's going to feel like Molly is actually here."

With this she drops to her knees and lets out an earsplitting wail. She rocks back and forth on the cement, clutching at her chest as if her heart is going to fall out. When the keening finally stops, everyone in the area applauds. Sarah takes a bow and grins at me.

"See?" she asks.

"Totally," I answer, clapping awkwardly so she isn't offended. I point to her streaked cheeks. "Did they have mascara back in Sweet Molly's day?"

Sarah shrugs. "Dunno. The face painter said we need to do this to demonstrate her grief." She snorts. "Like I need help with that."

"Mm-hmm," I say, the unsettling feeling growing. It started small, just a little crack. But now it feels like a giant chasm ready to swallow me, bones and all. "So, you auditioned for this, then?"

"Yup. Everyone did, pretty much. I mean, at least all the acting kids." She pushes her braids behind her shoulders so they hang down her back rather than over her shoulder. There are white ribbons woven into them, another detail I doubt is authentic. "Did you want to take my picture?"

I uncap my camera again, suddenly remembering what I'm here to do. "Yeah. Yeah, of course. Did you want to stand—"

I don't have a chance to finish my sentence. Sarah has skipped into the graveyard decorations set up in the town square. She lounges across a large fake headstone, the back of her arm pressed against her forehead dramatically.

"Do I look in anguish?" she asks.

Out of the corner of my eye, I see Joshua. He's sitting at a picnic table about ten feet away with a sketch pad open in front of him. With a smirk, he stands up and mimics Sarah's pose. He looks ridiculous.

"Oh yeah," I answer, stifling a laugh. "Total anguish."

I snap a few pictures of her, trying not to laugh the whole time. Each time she changes positions, so does Joshua. By the time I cap my camera lens again, my stomach hurts from bottled-up laughter.

〰〰

Forty minutes later, the parade is in full swing. It starts at the corner of Gaunt and Bony and winds all the way through downtown to the shoreline, and eventually, the lighthouse.

The bone key piano goes by first. It's old and warped looking, and unfortunately the music that comes out of it matches its appearance perfectly. The man playing it is the same person I've seen play it every month since I moved to Eastport. Mr. Figmont. He's tall and thin with a face sharper than a tack. He's also apparently tone-deaf.

Behind the bone key piano and its sharp pianist is a float with yet *another* graveyard scene on it. Only in this one, Sweet Molly isn't the focus. William Getty is. William "Graveyard" Getty is another one of Eastport's oldest legends. Rumor has it he owned the first coffin company here. According to the locals, he made gobs of money by building tiny coffins, then cutting the legs off the dead people so they'd fit in them.

Gross.

When the townsfolk found out what he was up to, they chased him into the ocean, where he drowned. Now the old sawmill where his lumber used to be cut is supposedly cursed, though I have no idea why or who decided that. Not that they care, anyway. It's all about the story. The darker, the better around here.

William's float teeters by in a cloud of dry-ice fog. The actor playing William creeps around the tombstones, pausing now and again to throw light-up necklaces and candy to the crowd. I snap a few pictures of his garish makeup, hoping at least one of them turns out to be something I can hand in.

When the music from his float drifts far enough away, a new song starts up. It sounds more like what I'd expect from a music box than a parade. I crane my neck to see the next float, freezing when I realize it isn't a float at all. It's Sarah as Sweet Molly. Unlike before, she isn't acting silly. She's serious. Her gown trails behind her as she marches solemnly down the street, her small hands clasped around a bouquet of black flowers. She makes eye contact with people in the crowd, her expression perfectly lost and forlorn.

When she gets to me, she stops.

"You," she hisses, crooking a finger in my direction.

I take a step back. I know it's Sarah, but the moment feels so familiar. Like the old woman beckoning to me in my dream.

The woman standing next to me puts a hand on my back and shoves me toward Sarah. "She wants you to go with her! She's chosen you!"

Digging my heels into the pavement, I focus my camera on her. Maybe if I start taking pictures, Sarah will remember that I have a job to do here too, and she'll pick someone else for whatever this is.

I snap three or four pictures, the hair on the back of my neck raising when I realize Sarah isn't leaving. In fact, she's not moving at all.

THIRTEEN

For a moment, it feels as if time stops. The sounds of the parade fade away until the only thing I can hear is the hiss...Sarah's hiss. Her eyes are trained on me, wide and menacing.

"You," she says again. The raspy sound raises goose bumps on my skin.

At first, I think it's part of the act. Maybe this is the surprise the check-in woman mentioned. Then I notice the dark veins snaking across Sarah's throat. They bubble to the surface of her pale skin, spreading until they've overtaken her cheeks. Her eyes glaze over, slowly changing from their normal deep brown to white.

I gasp and stumble away from her. My back hits something solid. A person. I turn around, horrified to see that they're frozen. Mouth open in a shout, hands up like they were clapping. And they're not the only ones.

Everyone is frozen. Everyone except me and Sarah.

I catch sight of Emmie across the street. She's got her camera raised in front of her face like she's taking a picture. Only she's not. She's still, just like everyone else.

A hand clamps down on my wrist. Sarah. She's dragging me toward her, her eyes shifting from white to jet-black. Her mouth falls open in a silent scream and her grip on me tightens. I try to pull away but can't. Sarah-not-Sarah is too strong.

"Stop," she hisses. "Stop it."

"Stop what?" I cry out, tugging as hard as I can to escape her grip. "Please let go."

I catch movement out of the corner of my eye. It's Joshua. He stumbles into the middle of the street, his face ashen and his mouth open in shock.

"Joshua!" I scream. "Help me!"

He breaks into a run. Just as he gets close, there's a loud boom overhead. Cheers and applause fill my ears, and Sarah suddenly releases me. I fall backward, hitting the pavement with a painful thud. The sky is filled with bursts of light— pink, blue, green, and gold.

Fireworks.

"You okay, miss? Take my hand and I'll help you up." The man behind me is no longer frozen. He's extending a hand. I take it and stand on wobbly legs.

Sarah is still there, but she looks like herself again. Her face is twisted into a mask of concern.

"I'm fine," I say, but the tremor in my voice gives me away. I shuffle out of the crowd surrounding me and do the only thing I can think of. I run. Another round of fireworks goes off overhead. Parents *ooh* and *ahh*. Kids shriek with excitement. Meanwhile, all I can think about is getting away. Escaping, before she comes after me again.

I'm standing in a bathroom stall with my palms pressed against the door when I hear Emmie's voice.

"Mallory? Are you in here?"

I keep my hands firmly planted even though the door is locked and look through the crack. It looks like Emmie.

"I'm here," I say.

"Oh my gosh. What happened? Are you okay?" She walks over to my door and tries to open it.

"Don't!" I bark. "Stay back!"

Emmie takes a step back. I can't see her full face, but the one eye I can see through the crack is wide and startled.

"Mal...calm down. It's just me," she says in a gentle tone. "I don't know what happened out there, but I can help."

"You can't," I whimper. "She's after me. Just me."

"Who?" she asks.

I scrub my hands down my face. "I don't know. The old woman, I think. The one from the harbor. Ever since I saw her..." I don't finish my sentence. I can't. The tears are spilling out now, and my throat is thick with fear.

"Please open the door."

I shake my head even though she can't see me. "How do I know it's actually you? Sarah wasn't Sarah, and I don't know what to believe anymore. Am I even awake right now?"

Peering through the crack, I see Emmie grimace. "You're awake. I swear it. And would anyone other than me know that you're secretly afraid of Mickey Mouse?"

Watching her carefully for any sign that she's the old lady in Emmie's skin, I breathe a sigh of relief. No veins snaking up her throat. No change in eye color. No raspy voice. It's just Emmie.

I unlock the stall door and open it. "He's a giant mouse with a creepy voice. Anyone with half a brain should be afraid of him."

Laughing, she pulls me into a hug. "Let's get out of here. I got enough pictures early in the parade for both of us."

Wordlessly, I follow her out of the bathroom.

Joshua is standing outside. His blue eyes are stormy, and his mouth is turned down into a frown. "We need to talk."

FOURTEEN

Weaving in and out of the crowds feels a little like the last time I had a fever. I could hardly tell when I was awake and when I was asleep. Time passed in weird spurts and everything seemed foggy.

Joshua is gripping my elbow, tugging me along beside him. Emmie is right on our heels. "Where are we going? Stop yanking on her and talk to me!"

He stops in front of the laundromat and spins around. "I'm going to tell you the same thing I told Mallory. We *can't* talk here. We're going to my house."

"No way." Emmie grabs my other arm and pulls me backward. Joshua doesn't let go. I feel like a human wishbone about to break in half. "We don't know you. We're not going to your house."

Dropping my arm, Joshua inhales loudly. "I'm not a stranger, Em. I'm in two of your classes. You just never talk to me."

"Is that true?" I ask her. "Is he in two of your classes?"

"I guess," she stammers. "There are a lot of people in my classes. Besides, what does that matter? If we've never talked, then I don't know you. Neither of us do. Hello, *stranger danger*!"

Joshua bursts into laughter. "Fine. If you're so convinced I'm a creepy stranger, then where do you want to go? If not my house, then where? It's cold, Emmie, and Mallory should probably sit down."

Emmie looks at me and I shrug.

"Somewhere public," she finally replies. "That way if you do turn out to be a killer, there will be witnesses."

I can't help it. I laugh. Emmie watches a lot of *Criminal Minds* reruns, but Joshua wouldn't know that.

"Somewhere public?" he scoffs. "Everyone in this town is out looking for gossip right now! Do you really want to give it to them?"

"I think I already did," I mutter, rubbing my sore tailbone. "Everyone probably saw me running away from the parade. They know something is up."

Suddenly I remember something. Everyone at the parade was frozen when the scary stuff was happening; everyone except for Joshua.

"You were moving. When everyone else was frozen, you came to help me," I start. "How did you do that?"

"I don't know," he admits.

"Wait, what? Frozen? What are you guys talking about?" Emmie asks, then blows a puff of warm air into her hands to warm them up. "I was at the same parade as you, and I didn't see anything weird until Mallory fell down and then ran away."

"That's because she didn't *want* you to see it," Joshua snaps.

"Who?" we ask in unison.

Just then, Bri bursts into the center of our triangle. She's panting and grinning from ear to ear.

"Omagosh! I didn't think I'd catch up with you guys!" She skids to a stop, suddenly realizing Joshua is with us. "Oh."

Awkward.

"Bri," I breathe out. "Hey."

"Hey yourself," she answers, a chilly note in her tone. "Where have you been? I've been texting you."

"Sick," Emmie answers for me. "Sorry, it was my job to tell you, but I got stuck babysitting Goob and forgot."

"Oh," Bri says, reaching out for my hand. "Are you better now?"

I nod, the lump in my throat growing. Is there anyone I haven't lied to lately? First my parents, then Emmie, and now Bri? I'm the worst.

"Yeah, thanks. This is Joshua, by the way. He's my neighbor."
Totally true and not at all suspicious. I hope, anyway. "We were
just going to get some hot chocolate at Cups and Cauldrons."

I hold my breath, hoping she doesn't want to join us.
I love Bri, I really do, but bringing her along will just make
things harder than they need to be.

"Ugh, now? Can't you wait like twenty minutes?" she
asks, her eyebrows wrinkling up. "I want to go but I need to
stay at the parade. It's important that I'm there until the very
end. You know, showing dedication and all."

"Dedication to what?" Joshua asks.

"The parade. *Duh.* I'm auditioning every single week to play
Sweet Molly in one of these. I want Mrs. Beckinsworth to see me
and know I'm committed to being the best girl in white possible!"

Joshua looks baffled, but he doesn't say anything else.
Instead he looks to me. "Up to you, Mallory. You're the one
who isn't...um, feeling great."

I turn back to Bri. I don't want to leave her out or hurt
her feelings any more than I already have but including her
is a bad idea. Bri is an actress through and through. Anything
she can use to get attention is up for grabs. That would include
what's happening to me right now. I wouldn't put it past her to
share all of this with her acting friends, and until I know what's
really going on, no one—and I mean *no one*—can know.

"Call me after the parade, okay?"

Bri's face falls. "You really can't wait?"

"I'm sorry," I give her a hug, but she stiffens. "Like Em said, I'm not feeling so hot."

With a nod, she walks away. Just when I think I'm in the clear, she turns back. "I'm not dumb, you know. I can tell when I'm not wanted."

She swipes at her eyes with the back of her sleeve and then vanishes back into the crowd.

My shoulders sag. Right now the only thing I have going for me is my friends, and I just hurt one of them. I feel like I'm caught up in a riptide, being dragged under the water no matter what I do.

"Don't feel bad," Emmie says.

"Easy for you to say. She's not going to be mad at you forever." I sniff and dry the tears pooling in the corners of my eyes. This day sucks.

"She might," Joshua says, then holds his hands up. "Don't yell at me. I just mean that even if she is mad, it's okay. You did the right thing. The less Bri knows, the safer she is."

It's his last statement that scares me. "Safer? Do you think we're in danger?"

Swallowing hard, Joshua meets my eyes. "I don't *think* we are. I *know* we are."

FIFTEEN

By the time we reach Cups and Cauldrons, I'm half frozen. Even early October in Eastport can be cold. The air whipping in from the ocean is frigid, and each gust is more bone-chilling than the last.

"Let's sit in the far back," Emmie suggests. "Less people to overhear this...*whatever* it is."

Joshua slides into the booth first. I hesitate. If I sit on the opposite side, it might seem like I don't trust him. But if I slide in next to him, then I actually have to sit beside him. Do I want to sit beside him?

I don't have time to keep thinking about it, because Emmie hip bumps me down onto the seat, grinning mischievously.

A waitress sidles up to the table and hands us some menus. "Can I get you kids something?"

Emmie and I both order a hot chocolate. Joshua orders a coffee.

"Coffee?" Emmie asks, her nose wrinkled up. "How mature."

"Forget the coffee, Em." I twist my body so that I'm facing Joshua. "I don't know how long I have before my parents start calling me to come help them, so we have to talk fast. Tell me what you meant earlier today at the check-in desk. You know, when you said you were watching me because the same thing happened to you."

Emmie's jaw drops. "Wait. *What* same thing happened to you?"

"The sleepwalking." Joshua studies the room, obviously double-checking to make sure no one is close enough to listen in. "I know you sleepwalked yesterday. I saw you."

Now it's my turn to be shocked. "Why didn't you stop me? I could've drowned in the ocean or been hit by a bus or something."

The waitress comes back and sets the drinks down in front of us one at a time. Joshua watches her, impatiently drumming his fingers on the table. The second she leaves, he dives into an explanation.

"I didn't see you until you were already back home. You were covered with sand and moving...I don't know...*zombie-like*. I could tell you weren't all there, you know?"

I cringe. Joshua's description of what I looked like that day is pretty much exactly how I imagined it. "And that same thing happened to you?"

He nods somberly. "I mean, the sleepwalking part did. I don't know what you did while you were sleepwalking, so that might not be the same."

"I dug holes."

Emmie snort laughs, then holds a hand up in apology. "Sorry. Not funny."

"I dug holes in the sand by the harbor," I continue, shooting Emmie a glare. "At first I thought I must've been looking for something, and maybe I was, but then last night I found this picture on my camera."

Taking the strap off my neck, I set my camera on the table and turn it on. "It's really unfocused, and I don't remember it, which means I must've taken it while I was sleepwalking."

Emmie isn't smiling anymore. "This is what you were talking about, huh? When you said something happened last night, but you didn't tell me what?"

"It's part of it, yeah. I didn't tell you about it this morning because I was scared. I thought if I just forgot about the stuff that happened and tried to move on, maybe it would all be over. Obviously, I was wrong."

The picture brightens my camera screen. I squint at it, stunned. "Where are the letters?"

Joshua leans in closer. "What letters? I see holes in the sand, but am I supposed to see letters?"

I yank the camera back toward me and press the magnify button. Once. Twice. Three times. No matter how I look at this picture, the word *stop* isn't visible anymore.

A trio of kids our age bursts through the door, startling me. They're all wearing the same hideous orange anniversary shirt. Their faces are painted with bats and pumpkins. I watch as the waitress seats them across the room, then glowers until they quiet down.

"Mallory," Emmie stretches her hand across the table and taps my arm. "You're shaking. Can you try to calm down and explain what's wrong?"

Taking a deep breath, I nod. "The picture of the holes—it looked different last night. The holes formed letters, and the letters formed a word. *Stop.*"

I look from Joshua to Emmie. "It was the third time I've heard that word in the past twenty-four hours."

Emmie looks skeptical. "Stop is a really common word, Mal. My parents are always screaming at me to stop something. *Stop using all the hot water. Stop eating all the M&M'S out of the trail mix. Stop telling your brother you're going to sell him on eBay.*"

She puts finger quotes around all of it, and I laugh despite my nerves. "I get that and I totally agree. It's just that those are normal circumstances. Each time I've heard it, it has been super abnormal. The first time was yesterday morning when I met the creepy old woman at the harbor—"

Joshua's eyes light up. "Wait. Old woman at the harbor? Can you describe her?"

"Sure. Wrinkled face, old, torn clothes, white—"

"Eyes?" he finishes.

I'm stunned into silence. "How did you know that?"

"Because she's been in my dreams at night. *Every* night."

For the first time, I notice the bags under his eyes. The skin is a light purple, just like mine. And he ordered coffee instead of hot chocolate. More caffeine. I guess I'm not the only one in Eastport struggling to sleep these days.

My heart thrums faster, and my hands go clammy. I wanted to hear what Joshua had to say, but now that he's sharing, I'm scared. More scared than I was before. How are we seeing the same woman in our dreams? And why are we both sleepwalking?

I take a sip of my cocoa, then sit back. "She's in my dreams too. They started shortly after I moved here, but they weren't every night."

"And they are now?" he prods.

I nod.

Emmie's face is sheet white. "How is it possible that you two are having the same dreams?"

"It's her," Joshua answers. "Whoever that old woman is, she's the one controlling our dreams. I'm sure of it."

"No," I say, shaking my head. "No one can control another person's dreams."

Joshua raises an eyebrow. "How else do you explain it?"

"I can't," I admit. "I know everyone here wants to believe in stuff like that, but there has to be a rational explanation. Right?"

Shrugging, Joshua runs a finger over his mug. "If there is, we need to find it soon." He looks off into the distance as if remembering something worrisome. "I didn't just dig when I sleepwalked. I got into the water."

"Wait. How do you know that?" Emmie poses. "I mean, we know what Mallory did. Mrs. James saw her digging, and she has that picture on her phone to prove it. Did anyone see you get into the water?"

"No, but when I woke up, I was drenched. My socks and shoes were filled with sand too."

"You *actually* could have drowned," I whisper.

All three of us go silent as the gravity of our situation sinks in. It's one thing to dig some holes when you're sleepwalking, but to get into the ocean? That's scary.

"What if the curses aren't all fake?" Joshua says. "I mean, they had to come from somewhere, right?"

Joshua and I look to Emmie. Out of the three of us, she's the only one who actually grew up here.

Emmie takes a sip of her hot chocolate and shakes her head. "Don't look at me. I've always thought the legends around here are stupid. If you believe them all, practically everywhere is either haunted or cursed."

"But," Joshua starts. "Just hear me out. What if one of them is real?"

Just the idea sends a full-body chill through me. Up until this moment, I believed the idea of something paranormal happening to me was ridiculous. Now that I hear Joshua's story, I'm having second thoughts. There's just so much I can't explain. *The old woman from my dreams showed up in real life. Everyone at the parade froze in time. Sarah turned into a monster in front of my eyes.*

I wrap my cold fingers around my cup, letting the warmth heat them. Being from Chicago, I've heard a lot of ghost stories. After all, the Windy City is also one of the most haunted cities. I guess I just never expected to believe any of them. Especially here.

"I've lived here my whole life and nothing like this has ever happened to me. If one or more of Eastport's curses is real, then why haven't I seen any evidence of it before now?" Emmie runs her index finger over the scrapes in the banged-up tabletop, then looks back to me. "No. A few weird things happening doesn't mean there's a real curse."

"I can't believe I'm saying this, but this wasn't just a *few* weird things. There are the dreams, the sleepwalking, the picture on my camera, the holes in the sand and last night... Last night, my closet filled with water." I fight off a shudder at the memory. "I searched the walls and ceiling. No way for that water to get in."

"No other explanation for all of this stuff," Joshua adds.

She laughs, but it's sarcastic. "Okay then, Sherlock. If you're so convinced there's a curse, then why is it only affecting you two?"

Joshua looks pained. "Because we're not from Eastport."

My head snaps back to look at him. I hadn't thought of that. "You think this stuff is happening because we weren't born here?"

"What other connection is there?" he asks.

I think on this, coming up with nothing. Other than our love of Converse, which doesn't seem like the kind of thing a vengeful spirit would care about, Joshua and I seem different. I do photography and he paints. I'm social and he's quiet. I drink hot chocolate, and he drinks coffee. The one thing we have in common is that neither of us grew up in Eastport.

Emmie downs the last of her drink. Her face is still white, but a blossom of color is beginning to stain her cheeks again. "I'm not saying I buy into any of this yet, but I'm up for helping you figure it out."

"Good," Joshua says. "Because if I don't start sleeping again soon, I might crack."

"Same," I mutter. Just then, my phone vibrates. "Right on cue. I gotta go help clean up."

Joshua and Emmie slide out of the booth with me. We exchange phone numbers and promise to text each other later. Joshua salutes me with a lopsided grin, then vanishes into the crowd milling around outside.

"Earth to Mal," Em says, shaking me.

"Yeah?" I turn to refocus on her, but it's too late. My best friend's lips are curled up into a knowing smile. I shove her lightly, laughing. "Don't say it. Just...don't."

We part ways and I head toward The Hill's tent. The hot chocolate may have warmed me up, but I still feel lousy. When the dreams first started, I never imagined it would turn into this. Now every corner I round makes me nervous. The old woman is everywhere and nowhere at once. The worst part is that she's in my head. Everything I know, or *thought* I knew, seems shaky now. Like our television during big storms—everything looks scrambled, and nothing, absolutely nothing, is clear.

SIXTEEN

The tent is already half empty when I get there. Janette is packing things up and Dad is carrying boxes to our ancient minivan.

"What should I do?" I ask.

Dad looks around and sighs. "Honestly, kiddo, I'm thinking you'd be more helpful at the restaurant. Can you head over there with Janette and I'll finish this up?"

"Sure thing." I pick up a tote bag filled with unused supplies and haul it over my shoulder. "Did you want to walk together, Janette?"

Rising up from behind the table, she swipes at the hair falling into her eyes. "You go ahead. I'm just gonna search the tent once more to make sure there's nothing left behind."

Probably a good idea. I don't know anything about what

it costs to run The Hill, but I do know that cooking supplies in general are expensive. Dad's favorite knife was over a hundred dollars!

The Hill comes into view a few short minutes later. Light flickers through the windows, probably candles. Mom likes to put them on the tables sometimes, says they're more atmospheric than just plain old overhead lights.

The bell above the door rings as I walk through. Mom is taking an order at a table in the front room. I sneak a peek into the back room, breathing a sigh of relief when I notice it isn't that busy. If I'm lucky, it will stay that way and they'll let me go home when Dad gets here.

Just as I reach the front counter, the bell rings again. A surge of voices fills the room.

Well, there goes that plan.

Mom is still hopping table to table, so I tie on an apron. Without Janette here, she won't be able to handle many more tables on her own.

"Welcome to The Hill. A table for five?"

"Yes, please," a man answers for the group. The sweatshirt that peeks out of his unbuttoned coat reads, *Eastport, MA. Our graveyards are better than yours.*

I fight off an eye roll.

"Did you want to sit in the front or back?" I ask, knowing

full well what their answer will be. No one sits in the front unless the back is full. Why would you when the casket wall is in the back?

"Back, please dear." The man nudges the rest of his group. They stop talking and follow me to the rear of the restaurant.

Setting their menus down, I pull out chairs so they can sit like Mom taught me. She's always said that coming here should be like an escape for the customers. They don't want the hassle of their own kitchen, so we need to do everything we can to make their experience here easier. Better.

"This is what I'm talking about," one of the women says, shrugging off her jacket. She runs a finger over the ghost-shaped napkin in front of her. "Lit candles. Ghost napkins. This place has personality!"

"Indeed," another woman agrees. "The Dentons have done a fine job."

I feel a strange surge of pride. My parents worked hard on this place. They still do. It's nice to hear people say good things about it.

After snagging a pitcher of water, I make my way around the table filling glasses. The conversation has shifted from The Hill to the parade. Whoever these people are, they seem to have had a lot to do with planning it.

I set the first two bowls of chili on the table, stopping

when the man snags my sleeve. "I hope you got out of here some today for the parade."

"I actually took pictures of it for my school, Harbor Point."

"A Pointer!" One of the women claps enthusiastically. "My son graduated from there a few years ago, and I have another son there now. So, you're studying photography, then?"

"Yes," I answer. "It's a great program."

I think she might want me to ask who her son is, but I really don't want to. He could be younger than me and if I show any interest, she'll ask me to be his big buddy at school. Walk him to the cafeteria and all that. I like kids, but school is the one place I don't have to interact with them a ton. Unlike here at the restaurant, where I spend a ton of time wiping down high chairs and cleaning up the food they throw on the floor.

"Indeed, it is. So glad we have you talented students covering all of the festivities. Especially this month!" She takes a sip of her water. "All of this good press will add up to a lot of visitors the weekend of the anniversary celebration. Mark my words."

The anniversary celebration. Ugh. Imagining another, even bigger Eastport parade makes me think of Sarah all over again. Her raspy voice. Her eyes. The way she'd grabbed me and refused to let go.

I break away from the table with a polite smile. Once I get far enough away, I focus on breathing. Good thoughts in, and bad thoughts out... I've only done yoga a few times with my mom, but I learned how important the breathing is. Right now, it feels like the only thing keeping me from breaking down.

When I feel better, I deliver some food to a few other tables, then circle back around to the bigger group.

"Ready to order?"

They all start talking at once. After their laughter dies down, they spit out their requests one at a time. I'm feeling better until one of the men asks me if I enjoyed the surprise at the parade.

"Surprise?" For some reason, the question sounds ominous. A cold trickle of dread rushes down my back. Is it a trick? Is he actually the old woman, disguised again? I look at him closely, watching for any change in his eyes.

"Yes, surprise!" he crows. "The fireworks? Surely you saw them. This is our first time using them, and we hoped they'd make an impression."

I let out a nervous laugh. "Oh! Yes, the fireworks. They were awesome."

He pounds on the table, making the silverware jump. "See? *Awesome*. I told you it was a great idea!"

The bell at the pickup counter dings. That means someone's food is ready. Mom sweeps into the room with it a moment later, expertly balancing a full tray on her palm and shoulder. I finish taking my table's orders while she launches into her monologue.

"They say it happened right there," she says, pointing dramatically at the man I was just talking to. Mom sweeps across the room, pausing right next to. "Are you aware of what happened here those many years ago, Mr. Hibble?"

He smiles broadly. "Indeed, I am. But I think I can speak for the rest of the council, here, when I say I'd *love* to hear the story again."

The council. So, this is the group of people responsible for making this whole month unbearable in Eastport? I struggle to keep a smile on my face even though I'd like to punch Mr. Hibble. All of them, actually. Don't they realize this is a town where people live and not a theme park? If it wasn't for their stupid ideas, maybe my parents could own a normal restaurant. Serve normal food. Tell normal stories.

I excuse myself to put their orders in. Really, I just need to get away. If it wasn't for the council, the parade today wouldn't have even happened. That means Sarah wouldn't have turned into scary not-Sarah. Today would have been the new day, the better day I wanted.

They ruined everything.

SEVENTEEN

I'm half dead when the evening rush finally settles down. Even after Dad and Janette arrived, it was too busy for me to leave. So, instead I served plate after plate of Poltergeist Penne—one of the restaurant's most popular things. Really, it's just penne pasta in a creamy red sauce with onion and red pepper flakes, but people love it. Almost as much as they love Mom's storytelling, which has been nonstop since I got here.

Blah.

Dropping another set of dirty dishes off in the kitchen window, I look toward the door longingly.

"Hoping to make a break for it?" Janette asks, skipping over. Her blond ponytail swishes around behind her, making her look like a little kid even though she already graduated college.

"You have no idea."

"Hmm. Maybe we can make that happen. The crowd is thinning out. And I'm saving up for a new espresso machine, so I don't really want to share the tips tonight if I don't have to," she says with a sly smile.

A glimmer of hope. "Really? Are you sure? You've been working nonstop since morning."

"I'm fine. Trust me. I have tomorrow off, so I can sleep as much as I want."

I must look excited because she laughs.

"Calm down. We gotta play it cool. Here's what we're going to do. You tell your parents you have homework to do." She pauses and narrows her eyes on me. "Do you have homework to do?"

I shake my head no.

"Whatever. Pretend you have *tons*. Then I'll drop some hints about tips being good today and how I need as many I can get. Sound good?"

I'm so grateful I hug her. "Thank you, thank you, thank you!"

Janette laughs and snaps a dish towel in my direction. "Okay. Beat it, then. Go tell them now and get out of here."

I don't wait for her to tell me twice. I need to get together with Joshua and Emmie again as soon as possible. I also need to talk to Bri. I feel terrible about what happened earlier today. We hurt her feelings even if we didn't mean to, and I have to fix that.

The walk home is cold. With the sun fully set, the streets are dark, and the wind has picked up. Without being able to see all the multicolored leaves on the trees it isn't nearly as pretty either. Between the tourists, the parades, and the cold, I've decided Eastport just plain sucks in the fall.

Pulling the hood of my coat up, I cinch it tightly around my throat. I'll be home soon. And when I get there, I'll text Bri and say sorry. Maybe I'll even send her some cookies from the bakery. Anything to make up for hurting her feelings.

I'm just rounding the corner by Crackinaw Cemetery when I hear rustling behind me. Stopping, I spin around and squint into the darkness. Thanks to a nearby porch light, I can make out enough to see that the street is empty.

At least it looks that way.

Taking a steadying breath, I turn back around and start walking. A few steps later, I hear it again. The rustling. I go still, afraid to keep walking but even more afraid to turn around.

Could it be her again? The old woman?

At this point anything is possible. In the past twenty-four

hours, more strange things have happened to me than in all my twelve years combined. And they're all connected to *her*.

I quickly run through my list of options. My house is too far away. By the time I got there, whoever is behind me will have already caught up. And the windows of the houses on this street are dark, like no one is home.

I'm alone.

I'm alone and apparently about to croak.

The rustling sound behind me turns into footsteps. I switch from a brisk walk to a full-on run. Without thinking, I turn sharply and pass through the graveyard gates. It might seem like the dumbest place to hide, but I'm betting that whoever is following me doesn't know this cemetery as well as I do. Thanks to several games of hide-and-seek in here, I know every creepy little hidey-hole there is. There are plenty of hiding spots, but you'd never find them in the dark if you don't know where you're going.

My breath comes out in white puffs as I round corner after dark corner. I leave the paved path, weaving in and out of gravestones until I reach what I was looking for—a cluster of tombs. Putting my hands out, I feel my way around them until I bump into a large circular handle. I plant my feet and tug. Slowly, it creaks open. In a flash I've slipped inside and shut it again.

Crouching down, I try to slow down my breathing.

I'm also try not to think about the fact that I'm hiding in a mausoleum.

Next to multiple dead people.

In the dark.

Maybe I should've just stayed at the restaurant.

I fumble around in my jacket pockets until I find my cell phone. Flipping on the light, I shine it around the small room. There's a stained glass window on one end, a marble bench, and six names etched into the walls. That means six people are entombed in this little building. *Six*.

My breathing grows more ragged. This is exactly why I didn't want to live here. I'm just not built for it. Maybe the people who grew up here are used to this kind of stuff, but I'm not.

A crunch outside breaks the silence. I hold my breath and switch off the phone light. Another crunch. Pressing my face to the crack in the side of the door, I peer out. Panic grips me as I catch movement in the shadows. Even through the darkness I can see something shifting on the path in between the mausoleums.

I scramble into the corner and squeeze my eyes shut. The footsteps start up again. They draw closer. Closer. I cover my mouth with my hand to stay as quiet as possible. When the footsteps stop, my heart nearly does as well. They're *right* outside. A low *wheeze-hiss, wheeze-hiss* fills the air.

Then the door bursts open.

EIGHTEEN

Something flies into my face. Leaves. I frantically swat them away, then spit out the crunchy bits that got stuck in my lips and press deeper into the corner. I'm trapped. Trapped and half blinded by shrubbery.

Wheeze-hiss. Wheeze-hiss.

The rasping starts up again, and the shadow standing in the doorway hunches over. This is it. My final moments on earth, and I'm spending them curled up like a pill bug on the floor of a tomb. How pathetic.

"I know you're in there," the shadow shouts.

I freeze. *That voice.* It's familiar.

Lifting my phone up again, I turn on the flashlight and shine it toward the shadow. The person in the doorway instinctively shields their eyes from the light. The second they drop their arm, I realize my suspicion is correct.

Messy blonde hair. Bright blue eyes. Custom Converse high-tops.

"Joshua!" I scream, still huddled into the corner like the chicken I am. "What are you doing?"

He holds up one hand while the other fishes around in his pocket. Within moments, he pulls out something red. An inhaler. As he inhales the first puff, I hear the wheeze-hiss again.

"Asthma? I was running from an asthmatic stalker this whole time?" I fume. Standing up, I brush off my jeans. They're covered in dirt, and I'm still shaking. Even worse, my temper probably just disturbed the eternal rest of dozens of dead people. Talk about bad luck. "I thought I was about to die!"

"I'm sorry," he starts. "I didn't mean to scare you."

"What did you mean to do?" I demand. "You chased me into a graveyard, Joshua. That's... I don't even know what that is!"

"I didn't realize it was you! I swear." He sounds panicky now. Good. Let him be half as scared as I was.

Shouldering past him, I step out of the mausoleum. My foot sinks into a patch of mud. "And now you've messed up my shoes too! Gah!"

Joshua is raking his hands through his hair. It flops back over one eye. "Can you stop yelling at me for a minute so I can explain? *Please*?"

His tone stops me from storming off. Or throwing mud in his eye. Both of which sound good right now. "Talk."

"I thought you were her. The old woman."

Aaaaand, now I'm offended. "So, I look old and wrinkly to you?"

"It's dark, Mallory. Really dark. And you're wearing white." He gestures at my white coat. "Plus, you were acting sketchy."

I fold my arms over my chest. "Sketchy. Oh, no. Do not try to pin this on me. The only sketchy one here is you."

Joshua looks hurt. "I was trying to help."

Deep down, I know he was. This isn't about Joshua. It's about me. Me feeling scared and weak and powerless. The old woman has wormed her way into everything. I look down at my coat, realizing it's the only piece of clothing I'm wearing that shows up in the dark. If I saw it from a distance, and with my mind stuck on the mystery woman, I might've gotten scared too.

"You thought I was the old woman and you chased me anyway?" I ask, confused. Every time I've had an experience with her, I've been so afraid that I couldn't think about anything except escaping. "What were you planning to do? Ask her questions? Capture her?"

He presses his lips into a tight line. "I don't know what I

was going to do! Maybe just follow her to see where she goes or to look for other clues. I've been dealing with her longer than you, Mallory—pretty much since the day I moved here. I'm sick of it. I want her gone." With a loud sigh, he adds, "For you too."

My anger melts away. I could be misunderstanding him, but it seems like Joshua is saying he doesn't just want to help himself. He wants to help me. "I'm sorry I yelled at you."

"I'm sorry I scared you."

I lift my foot up and shine the light on it. "But you are helping me clean this shoe off, buddy."

"Deal," Joshua laughs, pulling a hat on. He looks around the graveyard, then shudders dramatically. "Let's get out of here before the *real* old woman shows up. This place gives me the creeps."

"It should. It's filled with dead people," I answer, following it up with a villainous laugh.

"Jeez, remind me not to get on your bad side."

"Too late," I tease. But really, I like Joshua. He's funny. Nice. And he has great taste in shoes.

Just then, he trips and stumbles over a log in the path.

So he's not coordinated. Whatever.

"What are you laughing at?" He gripes, kicking a blob of mud off his shoe.

I lift my dirty sneaker into the air, cracking up. "Twinsies!"

Joshua lets out a loud guffaw. I start laughing then, too, doubling over when I can't catch my breath.

"I didn't know you have asthma," I finally calm down enough to say.

"You didn't know *me* until this morning," he responds.

Facts.

"Is it bad? Because back there you sounded like a zombie or something."

The streetlights are bright enough for me to see him shrug. "It's not that bad. Not anymore. It used to be, though. I was in the hospital three times for breathing problems when I was younger."

I frown at the thought. Having a problem with homework is normal. Having a problem with your locker combination? Same. But having a problem with breathing just seems unfair.

"It's fine. Really. Only bothers me when I do stuff like chase people through graveyards," he chuckles.

Before I know it, we're standing in front of our houses. I look up at the darkened windows of mine, disappointed. If it slows down at the restaurant, either Mom or Dad will come home so I'm not by myself late at night. But sometimes it doesn't slow down, and they both have to stay. I hope it's not like that tonight. I don't feel like being alone.

"So, tomorrow?" He blows into his hands, then jams them into his pockets. "Can you meet up after school? We can compare experiences and maybe start figuring out how to stop all this."

"I think so. I just need to ask my parents. Hopefully they don't need me in the restaurant."

"Cool. Just text me when you know."

"Can I invite Em too?" I ask. "She's been disproving legends around here ever since I met her, and she's really good at figuring out mysteries."

He waggles his eyebrows. "I know. I heard about the whole Eastport Inn mess."

My eyes snap back to his. "How did you hear about that? I thought Emmie's family and the owners of the inn were the only ones who knew about her research."

"My mom heard about it at work," he responds. "I guess everyone there was talking about it."

I don't ask him where she works because it doesn't matter. The fact that she heard about Emmie's research on Mr. Gaunt means rumors spread around Eastport even faster than I thought. Whatever research we do to solve our little... ahem, *problem*...needs to be kept as private as possible or we'll be a headline in no time. And if that happens, we can kiss our chances of solving it goodbye.

"For real, though, invite Emmie," Joshua continues. "We need all the help we can get."

Boy, do we ever.

We part ways then, both of us heading into our own homes. Joshua waves just before he walks through his door. I notice his windows are dark too.

Hopefully we survive tonight.

NINETEEN

I wake up with a start. I'm cold, so cold. Reaching for my blanket, I groan when I can't find it. Must've fallen off the edge of my bed.

Opening my eyes slowly, I look up. The LED lights that cover my ceiling aren't there. Instead, there are stars. *Real* stars. Real stars and a real sky...and real uncomfortable things poking me in the ribs and legs.

I swallow and sit up, terrified. Large rocks are piled up around me. The bottom half of my pajamas is soaked and covered in sand. My feet are bare, and my toes are freezing. Teeth chattering, I rub at my goose bump covered arms.

Wind howls from every direction, and a bright light flashes. I follow its movement until I see where it's coming from. The lighthouse. I'm lying at the base of the lighthouse. I stand up on shaky legs and squint into the darkness.

How did I get here?

Lifting a foot, I wince at the collection of scrapes I can make out on the bottom. My fingernails are filled with sand and my eyes feel gritty. I stumble a few feet, then sit back down. Everything hurts and I'm scared.

"Mallory?" A voice comes from the darkness.

I scramble away, panicked. "Stay back!"

Snatching up a piece of driftwood, I frantically wave it into the pitch black. On my third swing, it collides with something—something that lets out a muffled oomph.

"Ow! What in the heck was that?"

I freeze. "Joshua?"

Silence. The light flashes across the area again, illuminating a boy-shaped thing a few feet away.

"Joshua, is that you?" I repeat, feeling around for him. That sounded like his voice.

"Ugh. You hit me in the shoulder, you jerk." The light flashes across him again. This time he's closer and holding his shoulder.

"I'm so sorry! I thought you were…"

"You thought I was her, didn't you?" He asks through chattering teeth.

I nod even though he can't see me. Tears fill my eyes.

The light flashes across us again, and I stiffen. I could see

Joshua more clearly that time. His pale sand-covered skin and baggy sweatpants. I could also see something behind him. No, *someone*.

"There's someone behind you. Joshua, someone is behind you!" I'm yelling, but the wind and waves drown out my voice.

The light is coming again, making the same circle it makes all night every night. This time when it lights up Joshua, I scream.

The old woman is standing directly behind him, her mottled green hands stretching out toward his throat. Black veins cover her skin, and her mouth is drawn into a grotesque smile of chipped and rotting teeth.

Tugging him away from her grasp, I lose my balance and fall backward. Pain shoots up my tailbone and into my thigh. Joshua tumbles down beside me. A singsong voice cuts through the howling wind. It hums the eeriest, most terrifying tune I think I've ever heard.

"Mallory, get up! Get up, we have to move. NOW!"

This time it's Joshua pulling me away. He's yanking on my arm so hard I'm afraid it's going to tear off. When I'm finally on my feet, we slide up and over rock after rock, their jagged edges cutting into our skin, and their wetness soaking through what little bits of dry clothing we have left. The cold has seeped into my bones and no matter how far we get from the lighthouse, I can still hear her humming.

Taunting.

Threatening.

We're on my porch, shaking and silent. My front door is hanging open. Same with Joshua's. Apparently we both got out of bed, snuck out the front door, and walked to the lighthouse in some kind of trance. A trance *she* put us in.

"It's real, isn't it?" I ask.

"You mean the curse? Yeah. I think it's safe to say it is pretty freaking real," he says, wiggling his bluish-tinged toes.

I shake my head, a bitter laugh escaping me. "It's ironic, isn't it? I don't even believe in this stuff!"

"You mean you *didn't* believe in this stuff. No choice now." His tone is grim.

I lay a hand on the doorknob, shivering as my skin touches the cold metal. "I'm scared, Joshua. Really scared. What do we do now? She's obviously targeting us, and the next time, we might not get away."

His eyes meet mine. "That's why we have to figure out who she is and what she wants. *Fast.*"

TWENTY

I walk into school feeling absolutely rotten. I woke up before my alarm went off and immediately thought of last night. The lighthouse. Joshua. The old woman and her creepy sea shanty. What a nightmare.

Fear pricks at me. Eastport has never felt like home to me, but things are so much worse now. It doesn't just feel like a spooky little town filled with odd people, anymore. It feels dangerous.

Shaking off my dark thoughts, I scan the hallway for Bri. There's no sign of her pink puffy jacket or button-covered backpack anywhere. I texted her before I went to bed last night and included a bunch of silly GIFs and emojis I knew she'd like. I thought it would help make up for yesterday, but I guess it didn't work because she never responded. Just thinking about it makes my heart hurt. Brianne was one of the first people to be nice to me here in Eastport. She's bubbly and outgoing, even to strangers. I'll always be thankful for that.

I catch a glimpse of her just as Emmie rushes in and wrestles me into a hug. "Did you hear?"

"Hear what?" I ask, untangling myself from her grip.

"Applications are out for photography spots."

When I don't react, her eyes widen. "For the anniversary celebration? C'mon, Mallory! It's a big deal. I know neither of us like the lame parades around here, but if we got those roles, it would make it easier to get into the upper school."

Ah. Now I get it. The best students at Harbor Point Middle School are usually accepted into Harbor Point Upper, which is small and elite. Emmie has had her sights set on that as long as I've known her.

"You *do* want to go to the same high school, right?" she asks pointedly.

"Of course, I do. I just wasn't thinking. I'll fill one out today." I'm just about to pull her aside so I can tell her about last night when she sprints off in the opposite direction, skidding at the end of the hall as she rounds the corner. Either Emmie snuck into her parents' coffee this morning, or she's *really* excited about this.

Too bad I can't be excited with her. Right now, all I can

think about is the old woman and the fear I felt last night on those rocks at the lighthouse. A few days ago, I would've laughed at the idea of something supernatural happening in this town. Now there's no doubt about it... At least one of the Eastport curses is real.

I turn around and immediately crash into Bri. Her long blond hair is in a braid down her back. It's the look that Emmie calls *The Elsa*.

"Bri!" I hug her before she vanishes again. I can't mess up this apology. "I'm so sorry. I need to explain...about yesterday."

She waves me off with a grin. "Water under the bridge."

Wait, what?

"You're not upset with me? Or Emmie?" I ask hesitantly. My mom always says don't borrow trouble. Pretty sure that means I shouldn't ask too many questions, but I'm confused. Yesterday, Bri was upset. Furious, actually. Now she seems normal. This might seem like good news, but in the world of middle-grade girls, it most definitely is not.

She laughs and I notice that she's wearing blush and pale pink lip gloss today.

"I was, but I get it. You guys were doing your photography thing. You know I think that stuff is boring anyway."

Oof. Little does she know that photography had nothing to do with what we were doing yesterday.

"Besides," she continues. "I don't care about any of that right now, because today is the day. I'm auditioning!"

With this she jumps up and down and shrieks excitedly. It's so shrill that I cover my ears. When she finally stops flapping around, I uncover them and laugh.

"So, you're not excited at all, then?"

Bri cracks up, shoving me playfully. "Cute. My time slot is at three thirty. I wish you could come watch, but they said it's a closed audition."

I do my best to look bummed. I already have plans after school, but I don't want her to know that. Bri is talking to me again and I don't want to mess that up. "And you're auditioning for?"

"I told you yesterday. Sweet Molly. *Duh.*" She side-eyes me. "There isn't anyone else I'd want to be. She's the star, after all."

She sure is. Unfortunately, not in a good way. Every acting girl in this school will be auditioning for that role. I don't get it. All this competition just to dress up in a flimsy white gown to walk down a street in cold, rainy weather? I tell myself even though I don't understand it, it's important to Bri. That means it has to be important to me.

"You'd be amazing in any role," I tell her.

"You think so? Ugh. I hope you're right. If I get this, then

I'll for sure get the lead in the next musical. I might even get an early offer for the upper school!"

Bri's excitement is making her yell again. Clusters of students stop what they're doing to turn and look at us. I hold a finger up to my lips in a *shhhh* gesture, but she keeps going.

"Think about it. You, me, and Emmie all in high school together? It would be *epic*."

"Epic," I repeat, but I'm not thinking about that. I'm thinking about the fact that Joshua has appeared at the end of the hall, and he does *not* look happy. Not that I'm surprised after what happened to us last night. Happy doesn't really exist in Eastport.

I squeeze her hands and smile. "You're going to do great. Call me right after you audition, okay?"

She nods and squeezes back, then skips off for first period. Joshua tips his head toward the library. I follow him.

The first bell rings, sending students scurrying out of the hallway. That's the warning that we all need to be in our classes in exactly five minutes from now.

"What's wrong?" I ask as soon as I'm close enough to Joshua. "You look worried. More worried than usual, I mean. Is it about last night?"

"I am worried," he admits, raking a hand through his messy hair. I briefly wonder if he has a hairbrush. "But no. It's not about that. Did you have any dreams last night?"

I shake my head. "After we sleepwalked? No. Why?"

He nervously shifts from foot to foot. "Me, neither. I don't know exactly why that's bothering me, but it is. I woke up with a bad feeling, like maybe that awesome night of sleep was a bad sign."

"We've seen bad signs, dude. Like an old woman trying to strangle you at the lighthouse in the middle of the night. Sleeping well doesn't seem like one of them."

Still, he looks unsettled. "That's the thing, though. Lately it seems like the creepy things have happened *more* often. The dreams too. When I didn't have one last night after we saw her, I started thinking."

I don't like the direction this is going. It seems like every time I get just a little bit comfortable, something ruins it.

"About what?" I ask, even though I'm terrified to hear his answer. Up until recently, I thought Joshua was really strange. Quiet and antisocial. Now I realize he's not strange at all. He's just a watcher. The kind of person who doesn't jump right into something but sits back and pays attention until he knows what's going on. That means Joshua knows a lot more than you think he does at first.

I wonder what he knows now.

"I can't stop thinking about that documentary they made us watch in science last year. The one on storm cells."

I remember that one. We were studying weather, and one of the videos showed entire houses being gobbled up by funnel clouds. Being from the Midwest, where tornadoes are common, I wasn't that shocked. But they don't happen around here as often, so the kids in my class were kinda freaked out.

"What do tornadoes have to do with our nightmares?" I ask with a half laugh.

Joshua doesn't laugh with me. Instead, he sighs. "The calm before the storm. They talked about it during the movie. It's the period of time right before a huge storm hits where everything is still. Sometimes it's so peaceful that it fools people into thinking the storm isn't coming, and they don't prepare."

Suddenly the leftover biscuits I ate this morning feel like a brick in my stomach. "So, you think us not having any dreams is the calm?"

His expression is dark. Scary.

"Yup. And if I'm right, that means we gotta figure something out quickly, because the storm is coming."

TWENTY-ONE

Joshua's warning haunts me all day.

The storm is coming.

Even though I haven't known him all that long, it feels like I have. He's not as skeptical as Emmie or as outgoing as Brianne, but he's special in his own way. Quiet until he needs to be loud. And I think this morning by the library was as loud as Joshua Bergen gets.

When the final bell rings, I make a run for my locker. I have homework in almost every subject, but that will have to wait. First, I need to find Emmie and fill her in. Then it's time to team up with Joshua to start solving this nightmare.

"Ew. You look rough," Emmie says. She's lounging against my locker. Her whole left hand is covered in ink, probably because her last class was history, and she swears it's the most boring hour of the day. "Who died?"

"No one. *Yet*," I answer, shoving the books I don't need into my locker and swapping out for the ones I will. "Can you still hang out now? Because we need to talk."

Her eyes crinkle up at my tone. "Sure. Where are we going?"

"My house. I'll text Joshua so he can walk with us." I pull out my phone, then groan. "I have to check with my parents first. I totally forgot to see if I have to work tonight."

Emmie slams my locker door for me. "It's a school night, Mal. Even if they say they need you, tell them you have too much homework. *Group* homework."

I guess it isn't a full lie. This research on the legends *is* homework in a way. And I *will* be doing it in a group. I fire off a quick text to my parents, saying I'm swamped and asking for the night off. Mom responds first.

No problem kiddo. School comes first.

Guilt creeps in, but I squash it down. Even though this isn't for school, it's important. If my parents knew what I've been going through, they'd feel terrible. I consider telling them again but remind myself that it's a bad idea. Mom and Dad are busy. Besides, the curses here are a big deal to them. They're why The Hill is making money. If they think I'm trying to poke holes in any of Eastport's legends like Emmie did, they'll be angry.

No, I have to leave them out of it.

Joshua texts me before I can text him.

Meet on front steps?

I respond with a simple yup, then motion for her to follow me. "Let's go. He's going to meet us out front."

She jogs to keep up with me. "Jeez, slow down! Are you okay?"

"No. I sleepwalked again last night. Joshua too. We ended up on the rocks by the lighthouse and she was there...the old woman."

Emmie looks rattled. She turns as if she's going a different direction. "You know, I *do* have a lot of math to do."

Snagging her elbow, I keep her close. "Ohhh, no you don't. We need you, Nancy Drew."

"I thought I was Sherlock Holmes," she laughs.

"You can be whoever you want as long as you help us crack this case!" I dodge groups of classmates, my mind racing in a million different directions. Bri is auditioning. I wish I could be outside her door, waiting to either cheer or cry with her. I hate that she's all alone and has no idea what's going on with me. It doesn't feel right.

We burst through the front doors into the gray afternoon. A light mist is falling. I spot Joshua sitting on the steps right away. He's looking off into the distance, apparently lost in thought. I walk up behind him and tap him on the head. Bad decision. Joshua jumps up like he's been shocked.

I hold my hands out, palms facing him like he's a rabid dog. Is this what I have to look forward to if things don't change? Years of being on edge in this freaky town?

"Sorry," I say. "Didn't mean to scare you."

"It's okay. Probably the caffeine anyway. Makes me jumpy." He laughs, but it's too loud. Too fake.

He's freaked out for sure.

"You know caffeine stunts growth, right?" Emmie asks as we cross the street and head toward my house.

I snort. "Does he look like he cares about that, Em? He's already," I pause and look him up and down. "How tall are you?"

"Five foot ten," Joshua answers. "But my mom is over six feet tall, so I think I still have some growing left if the coffee doesn't get me."

"Wow. Is she in the WNBA or what?" Emmie asks.

Joshua laughs. This time it's real. "Um, no. She does event planning stuff."

I imagine a super tall woman hanging a piñata for a little kid's birthday party and no one being able to reach it. Smothering my laugh, I try to refocus. "My parents are at work for a while still. On Mondays, the restaurant closes early, but they still won't be home until after seven."

"Perfect," says Emmie. "I'd offer my house, but unless

you guys want to sit inside a LEGO fort and constantly fight off the snot monster, it's probably not the best spot."

Joshua wrinkles up his face. "Mallory's house is fine."

With each step my fear grows. I try not to think about it, instead focusing on avoiding puddles. My newish pink-and-green Converse are already speckled with dirty water. I'm beginning to think I should've started collecting backpacks or makeup instead of shoes. The weather around here is bad news for them.

I unlock my front door and let Emmie and Joshua go in first. Emmie tosses her backpack in the corner like she always does and flops down on the couch. Joshua sets his bag down gently by the door and takes off his shoes.

"Are you trying to make me look bad, new guy?" Emmie asks, kicking her damp shoes into the corner.

"I'm *trying* to be polite," Joshua answers. He lines his shoes up neatly on the rug inside the front door. "I haven't been here before, remember?"

I curl up in the armchair and listen to them bicker. The more he defends himself to her, the funnier it gets. It isn't until Emmie launches a pillow in his direction that I realize what's happening. We're stalling.

"We better start figuring stuff out," I say, a cold pit of dread forming in my stomach. "Last night was horrible."

Joshua nods, the smile fading from his face. "I'm ready. As ready as I'll ever be, anyway."

Emmie leans forward and pulls her legs up underneath her. "Me too. Especially now that Mal told me you guys sleepwalked again."

"Well, you guys wanted proof." He shifts uncomfortably. "Proof that the old woman is responsible for everything happening to us. So, I guess last night was it. She's dangerous, and I can't shake the feeling that she's planning something much worse than what's happened so far."

His words chill me. "Maybe we should start by making a list of the clues we have." I walk over to the desk in the corner and pull out the drawer. Snagging a notebook and pen, I head back to my chair.

"I think I told you guys pretty much everything that has happened to me. The dreams, the old woman at the harbor, the holes I dug, the water in my closet, and then the parade." I tick things off on my fingers one at a time, then quickly scribble them down in the notebook so we don't forget them. "Oh, and then last night's sleepwalking."

Nightmares

Old woman

Water in closet

Stop

Parade

Sleepwalking to lighthouse

Joshua looks thoughtful. "The old woman you saw behind me last night—was she the same one from your dreams?"

"I think so," I answer, then change my mind. "No, I *know* so. It was her. The light flashed over her perfectly."

Joshua nods slowly. "So, this woman is controlling us when we're sleeping, making us have nightmares and sleep-walk. Why? Is she trying to tell us something?"

A memory rocks me. "Emmie, remember when we went back to the harbor, and I told you the old woman I saw asked, *Where is it*?"

"Yup. We thought that might have something to do with the fact that you were digging holes," Emmie answers.

"Exactly!" I say, but I don't know where I'm going with this. "We kind of forgot about that once I saw the picture on my camera and realized the holes spelled out the word *stop*."

"A lot of these things are similar to what has happened to me," Joshua starts. "Like the dreams. It sounds like the same old woman in my dreams, but I've never seen her in real life. Last night she was behind me, so I didn't get a look at her."

"You're lucky," I mutter. "At the harbor the first time I

saw her, she had white eyes. Then they turned black. Just like Sarah's at the parade."

Emmie sits up straighter. "That's it. That's our first *real* clue. Sarah."

"How do you figure?" Joshua asks. "Sarah doesn't seem to have anything to do with this."

"But what if she does? Sarah was playing a role in the parade. The role of Sweet Molly."

Just the words put me on edge. *Sweet Molly*. The one legend in this entire town that makes me uncomfortable. The others are silly, funny even. Not hers. It's tragic. I don't have any siblings, but if I did and they died because the town cared more about money than them, you better bet I'd curse everyone.

"Mallory?" Joshua says. "Are you okay?"

I look up at him, realizing the answer is no. I've tried so hard to ignore the feeling in my gut since we moved to Eastport and as of this moment, I'm done. Every time I look out my windows, my eyes are drawn to the lighthouse. Every time I see a Girl in White T-shirt or key chain, my stomach rolls. Every time someone recites the poem, I want to throw up.

What if that's what this is? What if this is Sweet Molly's curse?

"The l-lighthouse," I stammer. "According to the stories, that's where Molly supposedly vanished, right?" I ask.

Joshua and Emmie nod.

"And Joshua and I just woke up there after sleepwalking again. Right on the rocks where everyone claims she walked into the mist."

Emmie's eyes meet mine. "Now we're getting somewhere. Including Sarah playing Molly in the parade and everything that happened during it, this *could* be a second clue leading us to Sweet Molly."

"It has to be. There isn't a connection to any of the other Eastport curses," I say solemnly. Out of all the curses I've heard of in Eastport, this is the only one I've ever been rattled by. It's scary, and I hate the idea that Sweet Molly is the one doing all this. Even more, I hate that I don't know why.

TWENTY-TWO

The doorbell rings. All three of us stare at each other.

"Who is it?" Emmie hisses in my direction.

I gape at her. "How am I supposed to know? I can't see through doors!"

I wish I could, though.

"Maybe what Emmie meant was are you expecting anyone?" Joshua deadpans.

"You don't need to translate for me, Joshua," Emmie snaps.

Ding-dong.

A second ring. This time I stand up. The blanket I had draped over my lap falls to the floor. I pace back and forth, my whole body already feeling shaky. "I should answer it, right? It's probably just the mailman or whatever."

"Totally," Joshua says. He doesn't stand though. Neither does Emmie. Instead they watch me. *Traitors.*

I stick my tongue out at them. "You know what? Fine. I'll get it. But I'll never forgive you guys if I get killed."

Crossing the room, I let my hand rest on the doorknob. I do a little countdown in my brain to prepare.

Three.

Two.

One.

I open the door and immediately see a pale face, white gown, and long wet strands of hair. Slamming it shut, I scream. Joshua and Emmie leap up from their spots and scramble to different corners of the room. I press my back against the door, my chest rising and falling so fast I think I might hyperventilate.

"Is it her?" Emmie shrieks. She's half in the living room and half in the kitchen at this point. Pretty sure if that doorbell rings just one more time, she'll make a break for it through the back door. "Is it the old woman?"

"I don't know," I say, cursing my quivering voice. What happened to being brave and figuring this mystery out on my own? "But it's not the mailman!"

"Well, who did it look like?" Joshua presses. He's wedged himself between the couch and the wall and looks ridiculous. I make a note never to pick him as a partner for hide-and-seek.

I go to answer his question, then realize the first person I thought of when opened the door wasn't the old woman.

It was Sweet Molly. "It looked like Molly. I was just thinking about her and thinking that all of this might have something to do with her legend. Do you think her...*ghost* or whatever can read minds?"

Emmie is fully in the kitchen now. Guess she doesn't remember she doesn't have any shoes on. If she actually tries to escape, she won't get far.

Three hard knocks echo in from the door. I flip around and make sure the dead bolt is locked. When I turn back to face the room, Joshua is crawling out from behind the couch. Unlike before, he doesn't look scared. He looks...amused?

"What are you smiling at?" I ask, annoyed.

He doesn't answer. Instead, he marches over to the door and nudges me out of the way. Before I can stop him, he unlocks the dead bolt.

I slam both palms against the door to keep it shut. "For real? You're going to get us all killed!"

"I'm not." He tries to open the door again, but this time I press my hip against it. "Relax, Mallory. It's not Sweet Molly."

"How do you know that?" I ask, panting with the effort of wrestling with him over the door.

"Because a ghost wouldn't ring the doorbell and then knock! Think about it."

I stare at him, briefly confused into silence. He's right.

Whoever is terrorizing us has already been in my house. They came in and filled my closet with water. No way they'd start knocking now. I ease the pressure off the door and take a step back.

When the door opens a second time, I don't see a ghost. I see Bri.

"What is going on?" She asks, frown lines creasing her thick white face paint. "Why did you just slam the door on me?"

I look her up and down, so relieved I could cry. Brianne is dressed up as Sweet Molly. Of course, she is. She just came from the audition.

"I thought you were...I thought," I stammer, unable finish my sentence. It seems so stupid now.

"She thought you were a ghost," Emmie finishes for me.

"Like you didn't!" I bark. "You ran like you were on fire, *Sherlock*."

Joshua bursts into laughter, pointing at Emmie. "You did. I didn't even know you could move that fast! Aren't you supposed to be the logical one here?"

Emmie slowly walks back into the living room. She brushes her hair off her shoulder, acting calm and collected. "I was just swept up in the moment is all."

"What moment?" Bri demands. "Seriously. What is going on? I've never seen you here before," she says, pointing at Josh.

"And you two are acting weird. Why do I feel like something is going on and no one wants me to know about it?"

Her lip quivers like she's about to cry. My heart clenches. If I don't fess up and include Brianne right now, our friendship is in real danger. She may never talk to me again.

I press the door open all the way. "Come in. I'll explain everything."

Twenty minutes later, and Brianne is still in shock. I've explained everything she missed in the past three days, only leaving out one thing: why I didn't tell her to begin with. Hopefully she won't ask.

"Whoa," she breathes out. "Just...whoa."

Whoa is right. I rub my eyes, wishing all of this would just go away. Back in Chicago, I didn't have to worry about legends and curses. I never would've even heard of Sweet Molly there.

"You guys believe that the Sweet Molly legend is true and she's, what, after you?" Brianne asks, her eyes wider than dinner plates.

I roll my shoulders. "When you put it that way, it sounds dumb."

"Not dumb," she replies. "Just unexpected. You normally seem so practical. And Emmie—"

She doesn't have to finish her sentence. I know exactly what she's about to say. Emmie is a skeptic through and through. She doesn't believe in any of the legends and never has. Then again, neither did I until one came after me.

"Even if that's true, something doesn't make sense," Bri adds. She looks up, her deep brown eyes a stark contrast to the eerie face paint. "The most popular legend of Sweet Molly is that if you cross her path by the lighthouse, she'll drag you into the water as revenge for her brother's death. But you two woke up at the lighthouse—the cursed spot—and she didn't drown you?"

"Obviously not," Joshua says, waving a hand over himself as if he's on display. Emmie cackles.

"Hold up. Isn't the whole town cursed, though?" Even though Mom focuses on the casket story at The Hill, I've heard her tell customers about Sweet Molly before. Many times. "I heard Molly cursed *all* of Eastport for letting Liam die."

"Me too," Joshua says without looking up from his phone. "Aaand we have a problem. It looks like there are a *lot* of different versions of the legend."

He flips his phone around for us to see. We crowd around it, staring at the dozens of websites about Sweet Molly and her many curses.

Great.

I lean back and sigh. "It's not like this is the only thing that doesn't make sense either. My gut tells me Sweet Molly is behind the stuff happening to us, but not all of the clues line up perfectly with her."

"Well, the fact that Sarah was playing Molly at the parade makes it seem like it's her, right? Same with you guys sleepwalking to the lighthouse. Those are both connections," Emmie answers, tapping on the word *parade* in my notebook. "And the harbor and holes in the sand can make sense. They're both by the spot where Liam's ship would have docked."

She's right. Although the docks have been rebuilt over time, the Eastport harbor is in the same location it was when Liam was a captain. There's a plaque on the wall of the bait shop that says the spot is a historic landmark.

"The word *stop*, though. That doesn't seem to connect to anything about Sweet Molly," I say, remembering how clear the letters were in the picture.

"The old lady too." Joshua tosses his phone onto the rug, frustrated. "She doesn't fit that legend. Sweet Molly was young and pretty. The girl in white. The lady I see in my dreams is...*not*."

"Right. If Sweet Molly is coming after us as part of her curse, then who is the old woman?" I pose. "It can't be Molly herself since she died young."

"No, she didn't," Bri says, a glint in her eyes. "That's just what they want you to think."

All eyes land on Bri. It's like she just took a sledgehammer to the conversation, and we have no idea what to do with the pieces.

TWENTY-THREE

"What are you talking about?" I ask. "All the legends say Sweet Molly cursed the town with her *last breath*. She died, Bri."

She's shaking her head, a tiny smile perched on her pale lips. "Nope. The legend *claims* she died. She lived in a nearby town until she was eighty-two."

Apparently, none of us know what to say, because no one speaks. I feel like our old printer that sometimes stops working when it has too many things to print. There are too many things in my brain right now. It has definitely stopped.

"How could you possibly know that?" Joshua asks.

"How could I not?" Brianne responds matter-of-factly. "It doesn't matter if the character I'm auditioning for is real or fake, I can't play them if I don't know anything about them."

"So, you've researched Molly?" Emmie leans forward, obviously excited.

Bri nods proudly. "Of course! If I'm going to be Molly, I have to understand Molly, you know? I've done *tons* of research, and I know for a fact that the legends about her are wrong. Totally wrong."

And here I thought she might make my situation worse. Forget three strikes, I have about a hundred at this point. I want to know what Bri knows. All of it. But first, I have something I have to say to her.

"I'm so sorry, Brianne. I shouldn't have left you out of this." I suck in a breath, suddenly nervous. "I was afraid you'd... I don't know...be dramatic about it?"

Bri's mouth turns down. "Dramatic? Like how?"

"I thought you might tell all the other acting kids or use it in a performance or whatever." I know admitting I was wrong is the right thing to do, but I also know how upset I would be if things were different and Bri kept something this big from me. "I was afraid."

"So, you didn't trust me," she says sadly.

"I was wrong."

It's only three words, but it must be enough, because Brianne leans in and wraps an arm around my shoulders. "It's okay. I haven't been the best friend lately either. I was so wrapped up in audition stuff that didn't even know this was happening to you."

I swipe at my damp eyes with my sleeve. "You couldn't have. I kept it a secret."

Lesson learned. Even when secrets seem like a good idea, they aren't. This one backfired. Big-time.

"And I *can* be a little dramatic sometimes," Brianne continues with a giggle.

Emmie grins. "You mean like the time you walked to the hospital because you had a sore arm and Google told you that's a symptom of a heart attack? Or the time you stuck lost dog posters all over Eastport because you hadn't seen Jimmy for an hour? Or the time—"

"Yeah, yeah," Brianne cuts her off, holding a hand up. "We get the picture."

I give Bri another hug, my heart bursting when Emmie joins in. I have the best friends in the world. They may be a little goofy, but we all are. Emmie is the skeptic. Brianne is the drama queen. And Joshua? He might not be a *best* friend yet, but I like him. More than I expected to.

As if on cue, Joshua clears his throat. I get the message. Making up with Bri is important, but if he's right and something big is about to happen, time is running out.

"Can could tell us what you learned about Molly? Like,

everything?" I ask, hoping Brianne has forgiven me enough to help us.

Brianne beams. "Yup. Get ready for a crash course in Molly Flanders McMulligan Marshall, guys, because I know a *lot*."

The living room is a flurry of excitement as Emmie grabs the notebook from me. Joshua drags a laptop out of his backpack. And Bri settles into the couch like she's about to tell a bedtime story. A really sinister bedtime story.

"So. It's true that Molly freaked out after Liam died. She was so sad that she couldn't bear to live in Eastport anymore because everything reminded her of him. Plus, she was angry with the people here."

Emmie scribbles furiously. Joshua must be taking notes too, because I hear the constant *click, click, clicking* of his keyboard. My heart is pounding so hard I can barely sit still. We're finally all working together, and I think we're on the edge of discovering something *big*.

"She was the only one who tried to save him, you know? I don't know if it's true, but I heard that Liam couldn't find his compass just before boarding the boat that day. Can you imagine? A ship captain without a compass?" Bri's tone is sad. Out of all the friends I've ever had, she's the most sensitive. Some people might think that's a negative. Not me. The kinder the better. "He didn't have a chance in that storm."

Emmie looks out the window like her mind is a million miles away. "No matter how good of a captain you are, you'd be a goner."

Joshua grimaces. Even though we already know how this story ends, it's still shocking to know so many people were okay with Liam leaving that day—without a compass *and* with a big storm brewing.

"Anyway, Molly packed up all her stuff and moved three towns over. She never talked to anyone from Eastport again." Brianne pulls a sweatshirt out of her bag and tugs it on over her gown. With her painted face and tattered skirt on the bottom half, she looks positively wild.

Joshua stops typing. "If she never talked to anyone from here again, how do we even know any of this is true? The internet didn't exist, so it's not like anyone could have tracked her down like people do now."

Brianne holds up a finger. "There's still evidence, though."

"Ooooh, now we're talking," Emmie says, rubbing her hands together villainously. "Maybe I'm not the only Sherlock Holmes in Eastport, after all!"

Opening her bag with a sly smile, Bri pulls out a folder. Inside are papers filled with black-and-white text. She takes one out and sets it on the coffee table, turning it around for the rest of us to look at. "This right here is all the proof we need that Sweet Molly didn't actually die or simply vanish on that shoreline."

We crowd around the papers. The top left has big letters in an old-looking font.

This is to certify that Arnold Chauncey Jr. and Molly Marshall were united in holy matrimony.

I stop reading there. "What is this?"

"A marriage certificate for Molly." Brianne runs her index finger across it, landing on the name *Molly Marshall.*

Joshua narrows his eyes on the document. "I thought her name was longer than that. Molly Fatlands McMuffin Marshall or whatever."

Emmie cackles. "*McMuffin*? Why would her middle name have been McMuffin, you weirdo?"

I snort. "Like *Fatlands* is a common middle name."

He rocks from side to side, bumping into both of our shoulders playfully. "You know what I mean. Seriously, what's up with the name? Are you sure that's even her?"

"One hundred percent," Molly answers confidently. "I got this from Mr. Andrews."

Mr. Andrews is the history teacher at Harbor Point. He's also a local historian who knows *everything* about Eastport. If he says that the Molly Marshall on this certificate is the same as Sweet Molly, I believe him.

"John Flanders and Seamus McMulligan were captains on the *Merriweather*," Joshua reads out loud, staring intently at an article on his laptop. "Looks like they quit working on the boat right before Liam took over."

Emmie's mouth is hanging open. "Wait. Molly's parents named her after boat captains? Who does that?"

"Maybe people who were really into boats?" I muse.

Bri slides the photocopy of the certificate back in the folder. "According to Mr. Andrews, back then the fishing boats were the most important thing in Eastport. Everyone worshipped the captains. And it wasn't unusual for children to be named after important people. Like the person who baptized them or an important figure in the community."

"No wonder Molly changed her name when she moved," I whisper. "She didn't want anything to do with the boat she blamed for her brother's death."

"Or the people," Emmie adds. "She cut ties completely."

"What about her parents?" I ask. "Did she cut ties with them too?"

Brianne's eyes darken. "She didn't have to. They died a year before Liam."

Quiet fills the room. For a moment, my fear of Sweet Molly is replaced with something else. Sadness. Molly had already lost her parents, then she lost Liam too. I didn't expect to feel anything except fear and annoyance today, but what Bri just told us changes everything. It also makes me more determined than ever to fix this. Not just for me and Joshua, but maybe for Molly too.

TWENTY-FOUR

I look back down at Bri's folder. "Is there anything else you know that might help us?"

"I don't think so. That was pretty much it." Bri scratches at her cheek, then groans as white paint flecks rain down on her sweatshirt. "Guys, I'm gonna have to go wash this stuff off soon. It's itching really badly."

"You can use my bathroom," I offer.

"Thanks!" She hops up and heads up the stairs, her long skirt dragging behind her.

"Get some sweatpants out of my dresser too. You look wacky," I laugh, then turn back to Joshua and Emmie. "Well, I wasn't expecting that."

"Me either," Joshua says. His tone is more somber than usual. Maybe he feels like I do.

"Besides how sad it is, there's something bothering me about all this," I start. "If Mr. Andrews knows all this stuff about Sweet Molly, why doesn't he talk about it? Why does he let everyone tell lies about her like they do?"

"The same reason I got grounded, Mal," Emmie huffs. "This town makes money off the legends, not the truth. I tried to tell the story behind the Eastport Inn and look at what happened. That's not even their biggest legend either."

"If people know the truth, the legends aren't as scary," I say.

"Right." Emmie shakes her head, clearly annoyed. "And if the legends aren't as scary, then they won't get as many tourists. Less tourists mean less money."

Joshua flops backward and lets his head rest against the couch so he's looking up at the ceiling.

"What are you thinking, Joshua?" I ask.

He shakes he head but doesn't look at me. "I don't know. I'm confused. I don't feel any better, even after hearing what Brianne said. I know there are some clues that don't fit Sweet Molly perfectly, but I'm *positive* it's her. She's after us, Mal, and I don't think it's because she's sad." He pauses, then meets my eyes. "I think it's because she's angry."

I think back on what happened to me at the harbor. The old woman. She sounded sad at first, but when I couldn't figure out what she wanted, she got mad. When I look up, I realize Joshua is still talking.

"It's not just the scary things that have happened to us, either. It's... it's a feeling."

"Like you're being watched," I say, my heart beginning to thump hard all over again.

He sits bolt upright. "You feel it too?"

"All the time. I've felt it on and off since I moved here." I meet his eyes, my nerves suddenly making my stomach feel like it's filled with a swarm of butterflies. "What if it's her watching us? What if the old woman we keep seeing in our dreams *is* Molly?"

The color drains from Emmie's face, making her freckles stand out even more. She looks from me to Joshua. "When I was researching the Eastport Inn, I got kinda distracted and ended up reading an article about ghosts in New England."

Ghosts? The butterflies in my stomach thrash harder.

"What did it say?" I finally find the guts to ask.

"It said that ghosts are sometimes people who are seeking revenge after death," she answers. "What if there really is a curse and the ghost of Sweet Molly is warning you guys?"

"I thought we just agreed that the curses aren't real," Joshua says, standing up. He paces in a tight circle in front of the couch. "Now we think they are again?"

"I don't know, but it makes sense, doesn't it? You and Mallory are new. You don't buy into the legend stuff. Do either one of you have an Eastport cup or key chain or any of that dumb stuff they sell in all the shops?"

Joshua shakes his head no.

"My parents got me a key chain, but I don't use it. Reminds me of how much I miss Chicago." I don't admit this very often. It feels mean to compare my new life to what my old life was, especially when my friends here are pretty great. I don't ever want them to feel like they aren't enough.

"See? It's this kind of thing that makes you two different from everyone else here. Maybe that's also what made you Molly's targets," Emmie pulls her hair back over one shoulder. It looks like a waterfall of red curls. "The question is, what does she want."

"So, we're actually kind of back to square one," I mumble, my hopes deflating more with every minute. We know more about Molly than we did before, but we still don't know how to get rid of her.

"Not really. If Emmie is right and Molly is targeting us as revenge for something—probably her brother's death—then we just have to put together the clues she left us. Right now, we don't have any idea what the holes you were digging were for, or what the word *stop* means."

I drop my head into my hands. This seems impossible. The picture I took at the harbor is mysteriously gone, at least the word I saw in it is. And the holes might still be there, but what will examining them do?

I'm about to tell them these clues seem like a dead end when our stupid chandelier begins flickering again. Once. Twice. Three times, and it's totally dark.

A scream rings out.

Brianne!

Jumping up, I head for the stairwell. Any other time, I might assume Bri saw a spider or didn't like the color of her lip gloss or something. But not today. Today I'm beginning to believe Emmie's theory—that the ghost of Sweet Molly is communicating with us. Warning us.

I clamor up the dim stairwell with Joshua and Emmie on my heels. Skidding to a stop at the top, I notice that the bathroom door is closed and there is light coming from beneath it. "I think Bri is in there!"

Joshua gets there first. He grips the doorknob and turns, but nothing happens. "It's locked!"

"Unlock the door, Bri!" I shout through the thick wood.

The voice that comes back is muffled.

"Are you hurt? What's happening?" I wait for a response, but there's nothing. No muffled voice. No Brianne.

"What do we do?" Emmie whispers. "Should I call the police or something?"

"And tell them she got locked in a bathroom?" Joshua gives up trying to turn the knob and takes a step back. "They won't come here for that. We need to get her out ourselves."

"Get away from the door, Bri! I'm going to break it down!" Joshua tilts forward and shoulders into the door.

I should have known better than to think a twelve-year-old boy was going to be able to break down a heavy wooden door. Joshua hits the door with a loud *thud* and falls backward. What's that saying my Grandpa Jim always used to use? Like a sack of potatoes? Yeah, he falls like that.

Joshua moans and rolls around. Emmie kneels down to check on him. Meanwhile, I try the knob again. This time, the door opens.

At first, I don't see anything. The bathroom looks empty. I take a hesitant step in.

"Bri?" My voice cracks.

The shower curtain shudders. I stare at it, frozen. It's just Brianne, right?

It moves again, confirming my suspicion.

It's not Bri.

I watch in horror as one mottled gray foot steps out of the bathtub. Then another. A gnarled hand reaches out and yanks the curtain fully open. It's the old woman. She's dripping wet, and her eyes are pitch black this time, like pools of ink. Her mouth falls open like she's going to scream. The sound that comes out though... It's anything but a scream. It's an evil rasp that sends a jolt of fear straight through me.

One at a time, the light bulbs above the sink explode. Thanks to the setting sun outside, we're in near complete darkness. Panicked, I take several steps back, tripping over Joshua and Emmie who are still crouched down behind me. We become a tangle of arms and legs, and after the second time I get kicked in the face, I realize Converse shoes are cute but painful.

I manage to flip over onto my hands and knees and crawl away. It's too dim to see the old woman anymore, but she's close. I can hear the rattle in her throat and feel the cold air rushing off of her. There's a smell too. *Death.*

Just as I'm thanking the universe for all the good times I've had up until this ridiculously bad moment, everything stops. The rattle-rasp. The cold air. The feeling that I'm about to die on the floor of my hallway.

"Guys?" The hallway light flips on. Bri looks down at me, her eyebrows tightly pinched together. "What happened?"

Joshua is lying flat on his back, hands pressed against his eyes. Emmie is up on her feet and braced against the wall. And I'm back in pill bug position.

I sit up and look around. "You didn't see her? The old woman?"

I know I sound hysterical, but I can't calm down. This is the second time the old woman has been here. *In my house.* It's bad enough that she stalks me when I'm walking around town, but this? This is too much.

"I didn't see anything except you guys lying on the floor, screaming," she answers, chewing on her lip nervously.

"I saw her," Emmie says, almost so quietly I don't hear her. "She was...awful. Stringy and gray with eyes so black they seemed like empty sockets."

Joshua rolls over onto his stomach, groaning. "Me too. I can't believe it. Did that really just happen?"

I expect Emmie to come up with some explanation because that's how she is. Something about how it could have been a figment of our imaginations or the shadows. Instead, she says "It did. And it will happen again if we don't figure out what Molly wants."

With this, Emmie peels herself off the wall. She brushes the bangs out of her eyes and takes in a deep breath. "Hold on. You were screaming, Bri. That's why we came up here. If you didn't see anyone just now, then what were you screaming about?"

Bri shifts from one foot to the other. Most of the white

paint has been scrubbed from her face, but a few small patches remain, making her look sickly. "There was a spider."

You have got to be kidding me.

I decide to give up and just curl back up into the pill bug position. I lean over and let my body weight pull me down, then rest my head against the thick carpet. If it wasn't for the faint gasp I hear come from Joshua, I'd probably stay there all night.

Sitting up a second time, I follow his line of vision into the bathroom. There, in the center of the broken light bulbs, is a message scrawled onto the mirror.

TWENTY-FIVE

"What is that?" I croak out.

The mirror is covered with writing. Jagged red letters streak down the glass.

REVERSE THE COURSE

I read it again. Then again. The words are dripping down the mirror now, looking way too much like blood. Panic settles in. This is another clue when we still haven't figured out what all the other ones mean.

"Reverse the course," Joshua reads out loud. "What does that even mean?"

"Ugh. I don't know." Snatching a towel off the bar on the wall, I turn on the sink and dip it in the stream of water. "This is my house. My house! Why did she come here?"

"She came here because she believes you can fix whatever

her problem is, Mallory." Emmie pauses, her eyes tracking my movements as I turn off the water and move toward the mirror. "Wait, what are you doing?"

"Cleaning this up." I reach out to scrub away the message, but she grabs my hand. Annoyed, I try to pull it back. "Em, let go."

"No." She wrestles my fingers from the towel and takes it from my hand. "If you wipe that off, you're ruining evidence."

Joshua looks unconvinced. "Evidence? It's not like we can take fingerprints or test for DNA. What are we really going to do with this?"

Emmie sets the wet towel out of reach. "I know we can't test for fingerprints and DNA. But we *can* take a picture of the message before we wipe it off."

And this is one of those moments I'm *super* impressed with my best friend. We're like peanut butter and jelly, Emmie and me. We're a team. When I'm freaking out, she's calm. When she's freaking out... Well, she doesn't freak out much, but if she did, I'd like to think I'd calm her down too.

"Yes!" I say, wrapping her into a giant bear hug and squeezing until she lets out a strangled *mmmph* sound. "We'll take a picture and then look at it later to see if anything has changed—like the holes in my other photo!"

"Exactly," Emmie crosses her arms over her chest, looking pleased with herself.

"I'll get your camera!" Bri races toward my bedroom. She's wearing a pair of my Harbor Point sweatpants and an oversized sweatshirt now. Even with the patches of paint left over on her face, she looks cute. And less like Sweet Molly, thank goodness.

"We have to wash this off as soon as I get a good picture of it, though. Otherwise my parents might see it." And if my parents see it, they'll start nosing around. Once they figure out what I'm up to, they might cause problems for me. And the last thing I need right now is more problems.

I turn back to the message on the mirror, realizing Joshua is quiet. Too quiet.

His jaw twitches as he stares at the dripping red letters. "Do you think this message has to do with the boat? The *Merriweather*? It sounds like something a captain would say."

"Reverse the course," Emmie says aloud. "I didn't think of that, but maybe. Reverse means to go backward, right?"

It definitely means to go backward. My father once reversed our minivan into a telephone pole. The bumper is still dented because of it.

"If this message has something to do with her brother's boat, then we're doomed," I say. "It sank two hundred years ago. There's no reversing now."

Bri rushes back into the bathroom and hands me my

camera. I take off the lens cap and get into a good position to take the picture. Once everything is focused, I snap several, just in case.

"You guys don't think that's actually blood, do you?" Bri asks, grimacing as she leans in toward the mirror to get a closer look.

"It's not blood. Fake blood, maybe. But real blood smells like metal." Emmie takes another sniff, then hops up on the counter. With her legs dangling over the edge she looks more like a little kid than the sleuthing machine she is. "This smells like chemicals."

I glance at the bathroom window, realizing it's pitch black outside. "So, what do we do now? We can't go investigate the holes. It's too dark to see anything. Maybe we just look around the house and see if Molly left any other clues here?"

"I'm game," Joshua says. "You guys cool with that?"

"I'm supposed to be home in twenty," Emmie says with a disappointed sigh. "Mom needs me to keep an eye on Goob while she cooks dinner."

"Goob?" Joshua's forehead scrunches up in confusion.

"The snot monster," I explain.

"Ohhhh," he says, immediately followed by, "Ew. I've never been so glad not to be an older brother as I am right now."

Emmie lets out a brittle laugh. "No kidding. It's totally

unfair. I'm the only one here who, after nearly being killed by a ghost, has to go and take care of a little demon."

Bri raises her hand. "Don't forget I have Jimmy."

"Jimmy is a fat old Chihuahua who sleeps twenty-three hours a day," I say, laughing loudly. "Pretty sure you can't compare him to Goober."

"He does fart a lot," Bri adds, as if that will earn her some sympathy. It works. My nose automatically wrinkles up just imagining those old dog farts.

"Gross," Emmie says, sticking out her tongue. "So, we're in agreement that we search the house really fast, then?"

Everyone nods. Everyone except for Bri. She's still standing in the bathroom doorway, looking lost.

"You don't have to look with us, Bri," I say softly. "If this is freaking you out or whatever."

She rolls her shoulders. "It's freaking me out, yeah. But I guess I'm more sad than anything. Sounds weird, but I kind of feel like I know Molly now. I did so much research on her life and all. I just feel bad for her."

Some people might think Bri is too sensitive. I think she's just right. And someday, Brianne O'Roarke is going to win every award an actress can win because she's talented *and* kind.

"We're going to fix this for her, Bri. I don't know how yet, but we will."

I look back at the mirror one final time, thinking about everything Molly lost. Her parents. Her brother. Her life. She didn't just leave Eastport all those years ago. She was chased away by the pain and the unfairness of it all. I make a pact with myself not to give up on this, no matter how scary it gets.

Then I take a deep breath and scrub the message off the mirror.

TWENTY-SIX

Our search turns up empty. No more clues. No sign of Sweet Molly.

I collapse on my bed, my brain swimming with thoughts. Some good, some bad. Most of them just confused. Joshua, Bri, and Emmie left about an hour ago, and I've checked the pictures on my camera about eight billion times since then. No change. The message on the mirror looks exactly the same in the picture as it did in the mirror.

C'mon Molly. Give me something to work with!

The wind picks up outside. It howls loudly, making it sound as if a pack of wolves has moved into my room. Crossing to look out the window, I glance out over my neighborhood. The streets are a patchwork of orange twinkle lights and Halloween decorations. Our neighbors across the street, the Jennings, have an entire fake graveyard in their front lawn—headstones and all. They've even dug up the grass in front of each tombstone to make it look fresh, like a coffin was just buried there. Gross.

My gaze catches on a light at the harbor. It's flickering, like someone walking with a lit candle. I reach for my camera, then use that to zoom in so the docks are magnified.

It *is* a candle!

The person holding it has their back to me. It's too dark to make out much, but I can clearly see one thing: they're wearing white.

Molly? What is she doing down at the docks again? I look back through the lens of my camera one more time. The figure is still there, weaving up and down the harbor like they're looking for something.

Looking for something.

A thought pops into my head. The first time I saw Molly at the harbor, when I thought she was Ms. Barry, she said, "Where is it?" I thought it seemed like it could be connected to me digging holes when I was sleepwalking. This could be proof that it is! If Sweet Molly is down there looking now, maybe I'd have a shot of finding whatever it is she's after and making her happy again. But only if I go there now. Alone. In the dark.

Setting my camera down, I try not to think about what I'm doing as I pull a sweatshirt over my head and grab shoes. I don't have time to text my friends about this, not if I want to get down there before she vanishes.

I reach my front door just as my parents pull into the driveway. No! Once they walk in, it will automatically be dinnertime and they won't want me to leave. I sprint to the side window and watch for the garage door to begin shutting, then slip out the front door. Once I can't see the house anymore, I text them so they don't worry.

B back soon.

The little dots pulse, telling me either Mom or Dad are texting back.

No prob, kiddo! We brought home Monstrous Meat Loaf!

My mouth waters at the thought of hot meat loaf. Guess I'm not one of those people who loses their appetite when they're nervous. I check the text thread one more time before putting my phone way. Hopefully they don't ask what that errand was when I get home. I don't want to lie anymore.

The wind gusts again, the distant tinkling of a wind chime echoing through the streets. It isn't meant to be creepy, but it is. When I reach the harbor, it's completely dark. I stop and keep my distance to be safe. I want to find what Molly is looking for, but I can't face her alone.

When I'm convinced she isn't here, I walk onto the dock, and turn in a circle. It's quiet. The boats that haven't been pulled out for winter are tethered and silently swaying back and forth on the waves. The Halloween lights are reflecting off the water. I breathe in the ocean air, tell myself to stay calm. It's dark out here, but darkness doesn't always mean danger. Back in Chicago, my favorite time of day was the hour just before I fell asleep. Since I stayed up later than Mom and Dad, the house was always quiet. Dark too. But not in a scary way. In a peaceful way.

I try to re-create that peaceful feeling right now. I imagine it like a force field, holding me safely inside. Then I turn on my phone flashlight and cross over to the sand where I dug while sleepwalking. Because of all the rain, the holes aren't really holes anymore. They're more like indentations in the sand.

A glint of light reflects off something near one of the sunken spots. I focus my beam on it and squint. It's no use. I'll have to get closer if I want to figure out what it is. When my feet don't want to move, I think of Joshua, how he's just as exhausted and scared as I am. And Emmie, whose brain will never let her rest again if we don't solve this mystery. And finally, Bri, who wants to see Sweet Molly happy for the first time in centuries.

Hopping off the edge of the dock, I trudge through the damp sand. When I reach the spot in question, I crouch down. The shiny bit is so small I can't believe I ever saw it from the dock. I reach down and grasp it, realizing it's part of something larger. A mostly buried something larger. Anchoring my phone under my chin so the light shines down on the spot, I start digging with both hands. My fingertips brush across a larger solid piece. I dig faster, tuning out the darkness, the wind chime, and the lapping of the water until I can get my fingers around the object. Pulling hard, I fall backward on my butt.

It's in my hands. Whatever the mystery item is, I got it!

I fumble around in the sand for the phone I dropped, shining the light on the object as quickly as I can. It's dirty, but I can tell that it's circular. There's cracked glass covering a symbol of some type. A star. I pump my fist in the air, thrilled. For once, I made some progress! I found something that might help us get out of this mess.

I shove the thing in my sweatshirt pouch and stand up. This has to be what Molly is looking for, right? I don't know how it connects to the message she left us on the mirror today, but it *was* in the spot where I was digging. Plus, it looks really old. If only she were here so I could try to give it back to her. I got brave enough to come here alone, I'm sure I would be brave enough to hand it to her alone.

At least I think I would.

With a disappointed sigh, I decide to head home. The best thing I can do right now is get home and wash this thing off, whatever it is. Then I'll text everyone a picture of it. They're going to be *so* excited.

TWENTY-SEVEN

"I think it's a compass," Emmie says, turning the mystery object over in her hands to examine the other side. "I've seen them in the maritime museum here. This star represented the different directions."

I agree with Emmie that it's a compass, but I'm still confused about the shape inside it. "There are four directions though—north, east, south, west. Why does this star have so many points? There are," I use my index finger to trace them. "Eight."

Joshua crams his head in between us to get closer to the compass. "There are letters on them, guys. Anyone have a magnifying glass?"

"Is anyone here ninety?" Bri asks with a laugh.

"Ha ha." He rolls his eyes. "The glass is cracked too badly

to see what the letters are for sure, so we can either guess or take it to someone who would know."

"No way," I say, putting a hand up. "We can't show this to anyone. If it's as old as I think it is, the museum would want it. No way people around here will let a group of seventh graders keep an important artifact."

"She's right," Emmie says. "If this is what Sweet Molly is after, then we have to protect it until we can give it to her."

Another group of students rush down the front steps of our school. I lean over to shield the compass with my body so they can't see it. We really should have found a safer spot to talk about this. I wanted to show them it to them before school, but Dad needed help early help at The Hill, so I ended up being late.

"What if this belonged to Liam," Joshua muses.

Bri reaches out to take it in her hands. Her mouth is gaping open in an *O* shape. "Omagosh. The compass he lost before his ship left the dock!"

"I don't get why Molly would want this now, though," I say.

"Maybe it's the only thing left of his and she just wants it back?" Joshua suggests. "I kept my dog's collar when he died a few years ago. I mean, I knew I'd never use it again, but I couldn't throw it out. It just didn't feel right."

Emmie stands up and paces. "I think he's on to something.

Molly probably just doesn't want anything of his left in the town that treated them so badly." She pauses, her expression going sour. "I'm not sure how this compass connects to the message on your mirror, though."

"I know. *Reverse the course.* I keep hoping something will come to me, but so far...nothing." I take the compass back from Bri and wrap the small towel around it again. Then I wedge it back into the front pocket of my backpack where I know it will be safe. "Honestly, though, does it matter? If this is what she wants, who cares how the clues connect? Let's just give this to her and be done with it."

"Agreed." Joshua stands and slings his backpack over his shoulders. "Anyone have a plan for doing that?"

Bri cackles. "You mean like a way to reach Sweet Molly?" She mimics talking on a telephone. "Hello, yes. I'd like to place an order for a two-hundred-year-old spirit."

Now it's Emmie who is laughing. She doubles over, then makes the same phone gesture against her ear, saying, "Hello! Delivery, please. One angry ghost with a side of revenge."

Joshua tries not to laugh and fails.

Meanwhile, I can't stop thinking about one thing: Molly was at the harbor right before I walked down there. Why didn't she see the compass and dig it up herself? It wasn't even fully buried.

I brush off the thought. I'm probably overthinking this. Maybe Sweet Molly has bad eyesight. I mean, she has been dead for a *long* time. Or maybe she left before she spotted it. Or maybe...

My mind snags on something.

Maybe this isn't the answer.

Of course, it is. It's a maritime compass! It was in one of the holes I was digging the day I sleepwalked. It's a clue, and it's the perfect clue to help us end this nightmare. I take out my camera and snap a close-up of it to be safe.

Ten minutes later, we're snuggled into a booth at The Hill ordering snacks. Seemed like a good idea to fill up before we try to contact Sweet Molly. Plus, the special today is Tormented Tortilla Soup—Emmie's favorite.

She slurps down another spoonful, her red curls spilling over her shoulders in waves. "For real. How are we going to reunite *you know who* with *you know what*?"

I look around the restaurant, laughing. "There's hardly anyone here, Em. I don't think you need to speak in code."

She points to a cluster of old men in the corner. "What about them? Hmmm?"

"One of them is asleep, and the other two have been

trying to finish their pie since we got here. Don't think they're a threat." Joshua smirks.

Mom sidles up to the table with a tray full of desserts. Today, she's got her hair up in a bun that she's covered in fake cobwebs. Her earrings are florescent green spiders. And her apron is one of her custom-made ones from Seances and Stitches. It's a graveyard theme.

Surprise, surprise.

"Here we go. Four slices of my Chilling Cherry Pie!" She sets the plates down in front of us. Each one has a fat slice of pie in the middle and a melting scoop of vanilla ice cream on the top.

"This looks amazing! Thank you!" Bri wastes no time in digging in. She rolls her eyes and sinks back into the booth. "It's incredible, Mrs. Denton!"

Mom looks pleased. "Well, thank you, Brianne. But remember you can call me Elaine. You're just too polite for your own good." She surveys the table. "Need anything else before I head into the back room for a bit?"

"We're good. Thanks, Mom." I look toward the back room, noticing that she has quite a few filled tables back there. "Do you need me to stay and help?"

"Nope. Janette is here, just changing in the back. And it's a school night, so we want you working on homework."

Or working on stopping a ghost who is trying to wreck my life
I think.

With this, Mom sweeps her arm out across her chest, wrapping herself in a black cape I didn't even notice she was wearing, and glides away.

The bell over the door tinkles, and a cold draft hits my back. I turn around, immediately recognizing the group that walked in. *The city council.* Just seeing them sours my mood.

Mr. Hibble enters first then begins shrugging out of his coat. The same two other men and two women are just behind him, including the lady who has a son at Harbor Point. Her eyes light up with recognition, and she immediately begins to wave at me. I awkwardly wave back, stopping when I catch movement out of the corner of my eye. Joshua is waving too.

"You know her?" I ask, confused.

He chuckles. "Of course I do. That's my mom."

TWENTY-EIGHT

"Your mom is on the city council?" I hiss. "You said she's an event planner!"

He looks like I just told him to eat glass. "Um, no. I told you she does event planning stuff."

"That's right. He did," Emmie says, shoveling the last bite of cherry pie into her mouth. "Why does it matter?"

I'm about to tell her why it matters when Joshua's mom walks up. How did I not notice how tall she is before now? I should've put two and two together.

"Joshua, I didn't know you'd be here after school. Or that you know this fine young lady."

She beams at me. I try not to glower. Just seeing the council puts me in a bad mood, and now that I know Joshua's mother is part of it, I kinda don't like her.

"Yeah," he says, obviously uncomfortable. "Mom, this is Mallory. She and I are working on a...project together."

A bubble of laughter bursts out of Bri, sending a chunk of partially chewed piecrust out onto the table. She covers her mouth, her cheeks reddening.

Emmie elbows her, and Bri shrinks back into her seat. "Sorry."

Grimacing, I turn back to Joshua's mom. "Nice to see you again. Mom is in the back right now, but I can seat you." I stand up to grab some menus, but she lays a hand on my shoulder and guides me back down.

"You're off duty right now, dear. Sit down and get that homework of yours done. We can seat ourselves." Joshua's mom smiles warmly. "See you at home, sweetie."

She ruffles Joshua's hair and walks away. He turns to face me, his stained cheeks a sign that he's embarrassed.

"What was that all about?" he whispers, looking back to make sure the group is far away. "Did my mom egg your house or something?"

"I just wish you'd told us she's on the city council. They're kind of the ones responsible for all this"—I wave my arms in the air—"stuff in Eastport. The parades, the anniversary celebration, the stupid shirts and—"

Joshua puts a hand on my arm, stopping me. "Chill out, Mallory. You're freaking out over nothing."

"It's not nothing," I say. "I didn't even want to move here. Now I'm stuck in this place where it's Halloween three hundred and sixty-five days a year!" I point a finger at him. "And I know it sounds mean, but your mom is part of the problem."

Joshua calmly sets down his fork. "She's just doing her job."

"Well, her job is making me miserable."

Deep down, I know none of this is his mother's fault. She's just doing her job, like he said. In fact, she's probably doing it really well, because Eastport has a *ton* of tourists. But I'm so tired and frustrated that for one second it felt good to blame someone. Someone real, and not a two-hundred-year-old ghost. If Joshua's mother wanted to, she could change things in Eastport. She could make it like a real, normal town.

"I'm sorry," I say, looking down at the table to avoid meeting Joshua's eyes. I'm sure he looks angry. I would.

When the silence at our table becomes too much, Bri clears her throat. "I think I know how we can get the compass back to Molly."

I keep my gaze fixed on the table. My stomach feels like it's tied in a bowline knot. I shouldn't have yelled at Joshua.

Emmie perks up beside me. "Oh? How?"

Tying her blond hair into a messy bun at the back of her head, Bri leans in conspiratorially. "Well, it would make sense that if she was already at the harbor looking for this, then she'll go back, right?"

"I guess," Joshua mumbles. It's the first thing he's said since I snapped at him. He doesn't sound happy. "And if we believe that the old woman *is* actually Sweet Molly, then Mallory saw her there the very first time too."

"That's right! So, why don't we take the compass there, and leave it out in the open where she can see it?" Bri proposes. "Maybe it doesn't have to be complicated, you know?"

Emmie is already shaking her head. "We can't leave a valuable antique at the harbor. Someone else could take it."

"Not if we watch to make sure that doesn't happen," Bri responds, raising an eyebrow. "There are a ton of spots right around the harbor where we could hide while we wait."

"Like a stakeout!" Emmie says, leaping out of her chair. "I'm in. I'm *so* in!"

I wish I could be as excited as her. Truth is, I'm scared. Waiting for the ghost of an angry, vengeful spirit to show up doesn't sound fun. It sounds like a recipe for disaster. I glance at the front window, noting that the sun is hanging low in the sky. We only have a couple of hours before sunset.

Bri jumps up and snatches her backpack off the floor. "Let's go now. If we're lucky, she'll show up, and—"

"Who will show up?" Janette asks.

"Oh, um," she stammers.

"Just a friend from school," I interrupt, hoping I can keep Janette from getting suspicious. "We're meeting her at the harbor." I try to wink as I say this, quickly realizing I've never winked before.

Janette's face scrunches up. "Are you okay? Your eye is twitching."

I sigh and my shoulders sink inward. "Yeah. It's nothing. Anyway, we should go. *To the harbor.*"

She waves me off with a laugh, then starts cleaning the plates off our table. "Yeah, yeah. To the harbor. See ya later, Mal." Janette carries the plates away. I can still hear her chuckling when she reaches the kitchen.

"Why did you tell her where we're going. *Over and over again*?" Emmie asks.

Bri snickers. "Seriously. It was like you were on repeat or something, Mal."

"It was smart," Joshua pipes up suddenly. "She told Janette so that if something happens and we are home late, someone will know where to come look for us."

I swing my head toward him, grateful. That's exactly why I did it. I should've known that if one of them was going to figure that out, it would be Joshua. Emmie definitely has the sleuthing edge, and Bri has the heart, but Joshua gets me.

Today he's wearing deep blue Converse shoes. They're identical to a pair I have at home. Just more proof that we're meant to be friends.

We exchange a smile, and my stomach slowly unknots. Hopefully that means he forgives me for being a jerk earlier.

The cloth ghosts hanging from the trees sway silently in the breeze. I look up and down the street, noticing that somehow, there are even more decorations than there were a day ago. Instead of the streetlights just being wrapped with black and orange ribbons, they all also have a large plastic pumpkin covering the light on top now. I imagine it glows when the streetlights turn on. Wow. They really should give up on calling this place Eastport and get on with using its real name: Halloweentown.

We're just passing Mrs. James's flower shop when I have an idea. "Hold on a second."

I leave them on the sidewalk and head into the store, immediately wishing I had a clothespin for my nose. The shop is quiet except for the soft humming of a large refrigerator-looking thing in the corner. It's completely glass so I can see the bouquets inside. Bold orange, red, and brown flowers tied up with Halloween ribbons and perched in delicate vases.

"Mallory!" Mrs. James walks in from what I would presume is her back room. We have one in the restaurant where we keep all the extra supplies. She walks up and takes my hands in hers. "What a lovely surprise! I've been worried about you."

It takes me a minute to figure out why she'd be worried, then I remember: the digging. Mrs. James told Mom she saw me digging at the harbor and I looked out of it.

I smile. "Thank you, but I'm okay. I got behind on homework and was really tired for a while."

Her eyes crinkle around the edges. "You poor thing. They work you kids too hard in school nowadays."

They do, but that's not why I'm here today. I scan the shelves, unsure of what I'm looking for. Except for the bouquets in the refrigerator thingy, everything looks so...old.

"I'm looking for something eye-catching," I settle on saying. "Like if I wanted someone to pay attention, what would I give them?"

Her smile is knowing. "Ahh. Like a boy, perhaps?"

Maybe letting her think that is the fastest way to get what I want right now. I honestly can't think of anything Joshua would want less than a bunch of flowers, but whatever. Not that I like him anyway.

"Maybe," I shrug coyly. "What would you suggest?"

She flits around the store, her round frame scooting between pots and plants at every turn. Stopping by the refrigerator, she rummages around. Then she pulls out a small bouquet that takes my breath away. It's in a dark green planter and features some flowers I've never seen. Bright white with deep purple spots like paint dripped from a can. They look exotic, definitely not like something I've seen in New England before.

"*Tricyrtis formosana*," she says. It sounds like a spell. "Or toad lily if you prefer."

What an ugly name for a pretty flower. I don't know as much as Bri about Sweet Molly, but I can't imagine she won't stop to look at these. They're so unique.

"How much are they?" I ask, suddenly aware of my pathetic bank account. Mom and Dad insisted that I have my own account here in Eastport, said it's good for learning responsibility. Problem is, it's much easier to hand over a plastic card to buy stuff than actual dollar bills.

Mrs. James snakes an arm around me and squeezes. She's surprisingly strong. "It's on the house, dear. I met Mr. James in high school and pined after him for years. Wish I'd had a way to get his attention!"

I laugh, imagining Mrs. James my age.

"Plus, you've brightened my day" she continues, handing me the bouquet. "Now...go get that boy!"

I hug her back. For the first time since I moved to

Eastport, I see Mrs. James for something other than a kooky old lady. She's sweet. She's also proud of her town and her flower shop, just like my parents feel about The Hill. And even though I don't like everything about working at the restaurant, I guess I'm proud of it too.

TWENTY-NINE

The harbor has already quieted down for the day. Back when fishing was the main industry in Eastport, I bet these docks were never quiet. Now instead of boats and fisherman coming in and out, there's just the occasional tourist snapping pictures and lounging in the sand.

Oh, and four amateur ghost hunters hoping to settle the score.

"Where do you think we should put it?" I ask, cradling the bouquet against my chest. "Maybe on one of the picnic tables over there, or do we want it right on the dock?"

Joshua looks up and down the space. "I feel like the dock is the most obvious spot, but can we leave it on the ground or is that too risky?"

"Risky how?" Emmie asks. "There's no one here but some seagulls."

"An old person could trip on it," Bri offers. When we all laugh, her mouth flops open. "I'm not joking! Aaron Helmson's grandma tripped over a vacuum sweeper cord and broke her hip!"

I pat her on the shoulder. "That's why we'll be watching. If someone other than Molly shows up, we'll warn them about it."

Stepping onto the dock, I pace around until I find the spot that feels like the middle. Setting the bouquet down, I let my backpack slip off my shoulder. When I have the compass out, I gently set it on the ground propped up against the vase. "How does that look? Obvious enough?"

"For sure. Where do we hide?" Bri steals a glance around. I giggle, thinking that when she's trying not to look suspicious, she looks *really* suspicious.

I notice a cluster of large rocks just to the right of the old bait shop. "How about behind those? They're close enough that we'll be able to see *and* run out quickly if we need to."

Everyone must agree, because they bolt for the rocks, leaving me behind. I quickly take a few pictures of the bouquet and compass. Maybe we'll never need them for anything, but it makes me feel better. Photography has always done that. There's something calming about seeing the world from the other side of a lens. From there, this bouquet looks pretty. And the compass isn't menacing.

When I have the shots I want, I jog to catch up with Joshua, Emmie, and Bri, crouching down as soon as I feel hidden.

Bri sits, immediately scowling. "Ugh! Nobody sit! The ground is wet!"

Setting his backpack down, Joshua tries to sit on top of it. The sound of things crunching inside makes me wince. "Yeah, this isn't going to be a comfortable stakeout. That's for sure."

"Is this dumb, guys?" I ask. "We pretty much just set a ghost trap made of flowers and a hunk of metal."

Now that I think about it, I feel stupid. It seems epically dumb. And dangerous.

"Plus, we've only been here like two minutes and my knees are already hurting," I shift my position, but it's no use. Squatting like this isn't going to work for long. I'm starting to understand why my grandparents are always complaining about their knees.

A twig snaps somewhere in the distance.

We go quiet. Bri's eyes grow about three sizes. And Emmie has a hand clamped down over her mouth, probably to keep herself from screaming and giving our hiding spot away. Joshua is frozen with his back pressed against the boulder. I can see his chest rising and falling quickly through his jacket.

Another snap. This time closer.

Don't move, I mouth to my friends. Then I waddle forward

slowly. I stop when I'm able to peer around the rocks. I can't see anything yet. Unfortunately, that includes the bouquet.

The dock is elevated just enough over where we are that it isn't visible and, of course, we forgot to double-check our view when we reached the rocks.

Sigh.

I ease backward, my brain scrambling for ideas. Pivoting on the balls of my feet, I look around for another spot we could dash to—somewhere with a better view of the dock. My eyes land on the cluster of bushes next to the picnic tables. They're perfect!

Gesturing at the bushes, I try to silently make Emmie, Bri, and Joshua understand my plan. I can tell they don't get it because they all look like they just got called on in class to answer a question they didn't even hear. I decide to lead the way and hope they follow.

I lean forward and peek out one more time to see if the path between the rocks and the bushes is clear. Only this time I do see something.

I see eyes.

Bulging, bloodshot eyes set into saggy gray skin.

Molly.

She shuffles toward us, both bony arms outstretched as if she's ready to snatch someone up. Me.

A scream erupts from my mouth. Joshua, Bri, and Emmie

leap up and scatter. I try to follow, but my foot gets caught on something. My backpack strap! I fall backward and kick it off, then try to crab-walk away from Molly.

It doesn't work. She follows me, gaining ground when I quit crab-walking long enough to get on my feet. When she's so close I can feel the cold air, a shout rings out.

"Hey!" Emmie is standing on the dock, waving the compass.

Molly stops. She turns and looks in Emmie's direction. Then she does the worst thing I could imagine. Well, next to killing me, anyway. She ignores Emmie. She ignores the compass!

"Nooo," I scream, still backpedaling. "That's what you want! Go get it!"

Please. Take it. Just take the compass and go. I force myself to stare into the pitch-black orbs that make up her eyes. Molly stops moving. At first, I think my two seconds of bravery did something, but then she opens her mouth. There's no scream. No rattle-rasp. Instead, her jaw continues to lower. And lower. It drops until Molly's mouth is open impossibly wide, like it unhinged entirely.

She's going to eat me. The idea makes me feel light-headed.

"Mallory! This way!" Joshua yells. I spin around long enough to see that he's by the bait shop. I sprint in that direction. Emmie and I reach the door at the same time. Joshua pulls us in, then slams it.

"Now, Bri!" he shouts. Bri shoves an old wooden desk in front of the door. "Gather anything you can. Block the door!"

Without thinking, I grab anything and everything that isn't attached and pile it on the desk. An old computer monitor. Empty bait buckets. A trash can. None of it is heavy, but it's all we have. Hopefully it will be enough. Hopefully the owners of the bait shop won't send us to jail for this later too.

When all the loose items in the room have been piled against the door, we move into the corner. I'm shaking so badly I can hardly stand. Tears sting at my eyes. It failed. The plan failed.

"Take these," Emmie hands each of us a fishing rod. They don't have reels or line on them. "If Molly comes in here, start poking her!"

Bri looks horrified. "I'm not going to stab Sweet Molly with a fishing pole. Besides, she's already dead, Emmie!"

"Well, what do you think we should do? Sit here and wait for her to come in and eat us or whatever?"

I inch toward the window and look out.

"We don't have to do anything," I announce. "She's... gone. She's just gone."

I'm part relieved, part heartbroken. I really believed this was our chance, our shot to end this once and for all. I guess I was wrong.

THIRTY

None of us are eager to run outside right away, so we take our time putting the bait shop back in order. Everyone is quiet, lost in their own thoughts. We failed. I failed. And now we're back at square one with no plan at all.

"I think that's everything," Joshua says, setting the monitor down and angling it so that it's facing the same direction it was in before we moved it. He turns a full circle. "Except for the lock I smashed to get in, it looks like we were never here."

Bri kicks at the broken lock. "How did you break this, anyway?"

He lifts up a chunk of rock from the floor. "I hit it with this. It was already in really bad shape."

Emmie snorts. "They need to upgrade their security here."

"To protect their old computer and some fishing poles?" I laugh.

"Good point!" she answers, lifting a plastic container filled with fake, rubber shrimp as evidence.

Stepping outside, Joshua waits for us to follow before putting the mostly broken lock back on the door. He scans the harbor, then swipes a hand over his forehead exaggeratedly. "Whew. That really was close. We're really lucky she didn't break through that door."

We are lucky. Molly was right on my heels when I turned and ran for the bait shop. I look back at the door, uneasiness poking at me.

There was no lock on it.

The wooden desk was small and light.

There was nothing heavy piled on top of it.

I look back at my friends, the seed of a strange thought planting itself in my mind. "I don't think she wanted to get in."

We stop walking right next to the cluster of rocks we'd originally hidden behind. A light drizzle is falling now and the already darkening sky has taken on a charcoal color. A few neighbors are out turning on their Halloween lights, but mostly everyone is inside now.

"She chased you, Mallory. Of course, she wanted in," Bri says.

Emmie and Joshua have walked back around the corner so they can see the bait shop door. Their expressions when they return tell me I'm right.

"There are windows," Joshua says, pulling his hood up over his head. A tuft of hair sticks out the front, getting slick with the rain. "You looked out one, remember? If she wanted in, why wouldn't she have broken one of those?"

"Or just shoved that door open. Any one of us could have done that." Emmie has her index finger pressed against her chin, now. I've started calling that her thinking pose because she does it so often. During tests, when she's trying to remember something...when she's solving a paranormal mystery.

Ugh. I can't believe we're trying to solve a paranormal mystery.

"Well, she didn't want the compass. We know that." I start walking toward home, grateful that all our houses are in the same section of Eastport. The wind spikes, blowing a wet leaf in my face. I swipe it away and pull my own hood up. "She looked right at Emmie, who was waving it around, and ignored her."

"I saw that," Bri says somberly. "I was really hoping she'd be happy. You know, take the compass and just...leave."

"We aren't that lucky," Emmie says, fishing the compass out of her jacket pocket and handing it back to me. "If she doesn't want her brother's compass, what does she want us to do with it? She led you to it, so now what?"

"I don't know," I admit.

We're standing in front of Bri's house now. Like every other home in Eastport, it's decked out. A fake witch is attached to the front, broom sticking out like she collided with the building. Large black spiders are set up all over the lawn. And hanging from the front porch is a life-sized mummy.

I give Bri a hug and so does Emmie. "Keep your phone on. I'll text if I think of anything."

She nods and trots into the house, dodging the mummy that is now swaying in the wind. The rain picks up, lashing my face with cold water. I make a mental note to move to California when I'm an adult. Or Florida. Somewhere warm.

We head toward the next house on our route, which is Emmie's. When we get there, her father is in the front yard, adjusting a trio of plastic ghosts. They're staked into the ground and supposed to look like they're toasting marshmallows by a fire. I smile. They're actually kind of cute, though I'll probably never admit it out loud.

Emmie waves at her dad from the street. "See you guys tomorrow at school. Maybe we can meet up after again."

Joshua and I agree. She runs up and gives her dad a fist

bump before running into the house. He waves at me and Joshua, then vanishes inside.

When we reach our houses, I'm fully soaked. Rain has come through my jacket and into my sweatshirt. My fingers are getting pruny, and I can't stop shaking. Might be a fireplace night.

We stop outside Joshua's house first. As usual, it's dark. Unlike all the other homes, there's only a few Halloween decorations scattered around—mostly plastic bones and a few fake cobwebs.

"Mom doesn't really have time to decorate," Joshua says, apparently reading my mind.

"She's too busy working on parades," I say. I try not to sound bitter, but it still comes out that way.

Joshua blinks at me. Rain drips off the tip of his nose. "She needs that job. When we moved here three years ago, she'd just gotten divorced from my dad. Everything was a mess. She cried all the time. I think she just wanted to make a new life here. A really different one. So, she worked hard and got elected to the city council. It makes her happy."

Oh. I look down at my mud-splattered shoes, feeling terrible. I was so hard on his mom. Mean, even.

"I didn't know any of that. I'm sorry, Joshua. I shouldn't have been judgy about her or the council." I wring my cold hands together. "I was just frustrated and looking for someone to blame."

When he doesn't answer, I look back at my house. It's dark inside too. "Wanna come in? I can start the fireplace and get us some snacks. My parents won't be home for a few hours still, and I bet your mom won't either."

"C'mon," I nudge him with my elbow. "I'm freezing, and don't pretend you aren't shivering. I can hear your teeth chattering."

Wordlessly, he follows me in. I say a silent thank-you. It's time for me to make things right.

After we get our wet coats hung up, I tell Joshua to put his shoes by the door and take his socks off.

"What do you want with my socks?" He asks. "You aren't secretly a witch, are you? Like, you're going to start a fire and toss them in a fire so you can hex me?"

"If I wanted to hex you, I'd have done it by now," I laugh. "I'm going to start a fire and we're going to dry our socks by it."

He arches an eyebrow. "We could just toss them in the dryer."

"What would be the fun in that?" I ask, adding a few more logs of wood then working to get the kindling lit.

It takes me a few tries, but eventually the flames grow. I sit back on my heels, savoring the warmth that spreads across my face. We had a wood-burning fireplace back in Chicago, so I've known how to start a fire for a long time. Plus, we used to go camping and without a campfire you can't have s'mores, so you better bet I figured it out.

"I've been thinking about the message. You know, the one Molly left on your bathroom mirror." Joshua holds both palms up to the fire, then rubs them together. "I think that's the key."

"Me too. How do we figure out what it means, though?"

He shrugs. "Not sure. Maybe we go back over all the clues we have and see if we missed something?" His eyes dart back to my backpack at the front door. "Can we look at the compass again?"

"Sure." I cross the room and dig it out of the pocket. Sitting back down in front of the fire, I set it on the floor in between us. I point at a jagged piece of metal near the top. "I think there used to be a lid on this. Looks like it broke off."

"Yeah. And this," he fingers a small metal loop. "Was probably the spot where Liam could attach a chain or something to it if he wanted to."

Joshua flips the compass over. The metal on the back is badly banged up. Between the dents and scratches, it's hard to see anything. Except...

"Are those letters?" I ask, narrowing my eyes on it. "I think they are! Can you read that?"

Lifting it up to his face, Joshua breathes on the metal and rubs it on his shirt. Then he starts to read out loud.

"Stay...the," he pauses, squinting harder. "Course? Stay the course?"

"Another clue with the word *course* in it." I take the compass from his hand and run my index finger over the inscription. I imagine someone giving this to Liam, having that engraved on the compass and believing this little scrap of metal would keep him safe. It's so sad that it couldn't.

"That has to be important, right?" Joshua stares at the fire.

"For sure. But I don't get what Molly wants us to do with that. We can't change the course of Liam's ship." The compass feels heavier now. More important. I wish I knew how, exactly.

My eyes land on the bookshelf, on the rows of books and the antique *Merriam-Webster Dictionary* my parents own. It was handed down from my great-grandmother and is pretty much just a collection of yellowing pages held together by a ratty cover, but it's cool. There are a lot of words we use now that aren't even in it. And there are words in it that we never use now. It's like a history of words.

A light bulb goes off. Suddenly I realize the message on the mirror and the compass may be connected after all.

THIRTY-ONE

I gasp. "Joshua! Every word has a bunch of different meanings. What if we aren't thinking about the right meaning for the word *course*?"

"What do you mean?"

I tick the thoughts off on my fingers just like I do with math. Even though we're supposed to be old enough *not* to use our fingers, I still do. It helps me keep track.

"One: Molly wasn't a sailor. She might not be using the word *course* the way Liam would have." I jump up from the floor and pull the dictionary down from the bookshelf. Along with it comes a face-full of dust. Coughing, I wave it away. "And two: Course is obviously used as a sailing word on the compass. But maybe Molly was using it differently on the mirror."

Joshua's eyes light up. "I didn't think about that. There are a ton of different ways that word can be used. Like in dinners or like a golf course..." he trails off, obviously thinking.

"Exactly!" I sit back down and open the book in front of us. The flames light up the pages more, giving them an eerie glow. "Here it is. *Course*."

Leaning over the book, Joshua reads quietly. "*The projected path of travel*."

Like the route for the *Merriweather*. I nod, encouraging him to keep going. There has to be something more here. There has to.

"*A part of a meal served at one time*." He pauses, then shakes his head. "I don't think Molly is leaving us clues about your parents' restaurant."

I roll my hand in the air, telling him to read. We're on to something. I can feel it.

"*A numbered process or succession*." He looks at me, his shoulders ticking up into a shrug. "Below this one it talks about medicine. Like a series of doses over time. I don't think this probably has anything to do with Liam or Molly either, do you?"

"No. Are there more?" I jitter my legs nervously, feeling antsy.

He turns the page. "*A chosen manner of conducting oneself: a way of acting*."

It's in this moment that Joshua's expression changes. It goes from excited and curious to...scared?

"What? Does it say something else?" The tone of my voice rises. I sound shrill and panicky. Probably because I am.

"The example below it reads *our wisest course is to retreat.*"

Retreat. Reverse. Act differently.

But who? Who does Molly want to act differently?

~~~~

Ten minutes later, and we're still sitting by the fire, dazed. The wood crackles, sending the flames higher just long enough to brighten our socks, still dangling limply from the mantel. I look out the window, my gaze lingering on our neighbor who appears to be dragging something large out of his garage. It looks like a person. I stand up and run to the window to get a closer look.

"What... What is that?" He lifts the person-shaped thing up, revealing that it's not a person. It's a doll. A life-sized doll. The face is painted white, and there are large tufts of hay sticking out from underneath the sleeves of the white gown it's wearing—Molly's gown. I'd recognize it anywhere. The neighbor made a Sweet Molly decoration.

I turn away in disgust. Joshua is at my side, his lips twisted in annoyance.

"Bri keeps saying she feels bad for Molly," I start. "I think I actually get it now."

The words from my mother's monologue at The Hill pop into my head. *They're angry and looking for revenge.* She's talking about the spirit of the person whose eternal rest was disturbed when the coffin burst through the dining room wall. But what about Molly's eternal rest? How can her spirit move on and be at peace when all of Eastport won't let her? She's on almost every key chain, coffee mug, and T-shirt they sell in this town. Now she's turned into a lawn decoration too?

The truth hits me in the face like an anchor. It's not the ship Molly wanted to reverse course, and it isn't an actual route she's talking about. *It's Eastport.* She wants the people of Eastport to act differently.

I point at the Sweet Molly doll, which is now standing upright in the center of my neighbor's fake graveyard. Its creepy, frowning mouth is drawn on in red lipstick. "Molly was never talking about her brother and his boat. She was talking about this town. The way they act."

"Eastport's course," Joshua whispers. "Her brother died tragically. And now this entire town celebrates it. They reenact it."

I think about the parades down Gaunt Street. How everyone gathers and cheers as a new actress each week pretends to be Molly. Moaning and wailing. *Grieving.* Eastport has made a big, big mistake, and I'm afraid if we can't convince them to fix it, Molly is going to lose what little bit of patience she has left and do something truly awful. But how? How can we possibly convince this town that what they're doing is wrong?

Joshua drops his head into his hands. When he looks back up, his hair is standing on end and his eyes are wrinkled at the edges. "You were right. About the council and my mom."

"No. She doesn't know, Joshua. None of them do. They don't see what they're doing to Molly. They just see the money they're making for Eastport."

Just then, I hear the sound of our side door opening. I crane my neck to see down the hall, relieved when I realize it's just Mom. She's dripping wet and carrying a brown bag. Probably dinner.

"Hey, Mal. Dad is staying back with Janette to close up the diner." She kicks her shoes off and comes down into the living room, stopping when she sees Joshua. "Well, hello again. Nice to see you, Joshua. I have some dinner waiting in the kitchen. Would you like to stay?"

Joshua smiles, but it doesn't quite reach his eyes. I know what he's thinking. How could anyone be hungry when we know what we have to do now? It seems impossible.

"I should get home but thank you." He stands up and grabs his socks.

"All right, but you're free to change your mind. There's plenty." She heads back into the kitchen with a grin.

Great. Now Mom thinks I like Joshua.

Do I like Joshua?

I turn back and look at him. His ocean blue eyes. His lightly freckled skin. His sock flying into my face.

Snapping back to reality, I bat the soggy sock away. "Gross! What are you doing?"

Joshua cackles and shoves it into his backpack. "Thanks to you and your wacky fireplace idea, my socks smell like roasted feet. Disgusting."

"Well, don't stick them in my face, you jerk." I walk him to the door and open it. "Can you to go school early tomorrow? We could meet up with Emmie and Bri and fill them in on all this."

"Yup." He slings the backpack over his shoulders and heads down the front steps. His house is still dark. Even though it would be awkward with Mom watching us like a hawk, I kinda wish Joshua was staying for dinner. These days, going home to an empty, dark house isn't fun. Not with a ghost after us. "I'll just walk with you."

Just as he reaches his door, Joshua tosses me the same goofy salute and crooked smile he did the day we met. The day of the parade. I'd give anything to turn back time so I never went to that stupid thing to begin with. Things weren't good before it, but they weren't *this* bad. Molly's dark eyes and gaping mouth pop into my head again, and I try to shake them out. We can't keep this up much longer. Running. Hiding. Hoping. Eventually Sweet Molly will catch us, and there's no telling what she'll do.

THIRTY-TWO

When Joshua and I reach the school the following morning, Emmie is already standing there. Even with a heavy coat on and a hoodie underneath, she's still shivering.

Joshua points to her head. "You have double hoods going on and you're still cold?"

"F-f-freezing!" she stammers, shifting from side to side to warm up. "Bri called me a few minutes ago and asked if we could meet her in the auditorium. The cast for the big anniversary celebration is being announced today, and she wants us to be there when she finds out if she got the role or not."

My stomach drops like I'm on a roller coaster. I don't want to think about the anniversary event. But I do want to be there for Bri.

"She still wants to do this? Even after all this stuff with Molly?" Joshua asks.

"She doesn't know everything yet. Not what we figured out last night after she went home," I tell him. "I texted her after you left, same as I did with Emmie, but she was busy. I tried video calling her too."

Emmie rubs her temples with a gloved hand. "I did the same. Ugh. Knowing what we know now, Bri being involved in this at all seems like it's only going to make Molly madder."

"Of course, it's going to make her madder!" Joshua says like it's the most obvious thing ever. "Just tell her she can't do it. That it's dangerous."

"You really don't know Bri at all, because it's not that simple, Joshua. She's really into acting. Like, it's everything to her. She said that this is the role of a lifetime." Emmie sighs.

"She keeps talking about her calling card and how this role would look great on it. I think it's like a résumé for actors and actresses," Emmie continues. "I don't know why she's working on this in seventh grade."

"There are seventh graders in movies," Joshua says. "If she's good, she's good. Still, it's not worth the risk."

He's right. I wish Bri had been auditioning for something that isn't connected to a ghost who wants revenge. I let the thought I've been trying to keep out of my mind finally slide in. *Maybe she won't get the part anyway.* I feel terrible rooting against one of my best friends, but it would be safer for her. For all of us. I cross my fingers and say a silent prayer. For once, I don't want Bri to succeed.

We can hear the commotion before we even see the auditorium doors. Inside, at least a hundred students are gathered in clusters. Bri is in the corner, wildly waving both arms in the air at us.

"They're going to post the list in less than five minutes," she says the second we reach her. She's so excited she sounds out of breath. "I'm so nervous. Like I actually feel like I could faint. Or throw up. Or both."

Joshua takes a step back. I laugh. Yet another thing I like about him. He doesn't mean to be funny. He just is.

"Are you sure this is a good idea, Bri? Just yesterday, Molly was"—I look around to make sure no one is listening, then lower my voice—"*chasing* us. And last night—"

"Last night we figured some stuff out," Josh finishes my sentence for me. "We don't think Molly likes the parades and reenactments very much. This role might make her angrier."

Still bouncing on the balls of her feet nervously, she nods. "Can we please not talk about this right now? We don't even know if I got the part. Besides, I really don't think a two-hundred-year-old ghost will care if I'm in a dumb small-town performance."

What I want to say is, *why do you care so much then*, but I don't. I said I was going to be a good friend to Bri and I am. Problem is, for the first time ever, being a good friend might mean *not* supporting her.

A woman steps out on the stage. Excited shrieks fill the air.

Bri grabs my arm and shakes it so hard I almost lose my balance. "This is it!"

"Everyone, please settle down," the woman says into the microphone. "I'm going to be posting the cast list in a moment. I'd like to request that you take turns viewing it in an orderly manner."

The crowd surges forward. Orderly manner, ha! They're going to go after that thing like a herd of rhinos.

The cast list is posted on a different wall than Bri expected. We're at the back of the group. I can't see the expressions of the first students to see it, but I can hear what they're yelling...

Brianne O'Roarke.

She got the part. Bri is going to be Sweet Molly in the big parade. She's surrounded by acting friends now, half of Harbor Point hugging her and cheering her on. The other half is in tears on a different side of the auditorium.

Meanwhile, I feel like I'm going to cry. Is this really happening? I glance at Joshua. His eyes are darker than the sky before a storm. This is bad.

"Bri, we really need to talk," I shout over the din, my stomach tying itself back into the knot I'm getting so used to.

When Bri is finally able to untangle herself from the chaos, she gestures for us to follow her backstage.

"Can you believe it?" she says, panting. "I can't. I just can't. I auditioned along with seniors for this!" She digs out her phone. "I have to call my mom!"

Emmie snatches the phone from her hands.

"Hey!" Bri says, her eyebrows wrinkling up. "What did you do that for?"

"Don't call your mom. Please. Just sit down and listen."

Scowling, Bri lowers down onto a large gray lump. I recognize it from the last performance. From a distance it looked just like a rock, but up close it's just a big hunk of painted wood. I look around the area, realizing I've never actually been backstage. It's interesting. There are storage containers filled with all sorts of props sitting around. The one marked *dining room scene* is filled with plates and cups. Another one, filled to the brim with dolls, has the words *kids room* written on it.

"We're proud of you, Bri," Emmie says. She's holding back, though. I think we all are. None of us want to tell Brianne the truth—that we're afraid her exciting new role is going to make things worse. "We really are. It's just that we think you should consider turning down the role."

Bri looks like someone just kicked her. "Turn down the role? Are you joking?"

I crouch down on top of another fake rock. Emmie and Joshua find two folding chairs they set out. The noise in the auditorium is finally quieting, but based on the way Bri's knees are bobbing up and down, it's clear she hasn't calmed down yet.

This isn't going to go well.

"Before you answer that, you need to know something. I have a plan. I'm going to play Molly different from everyone else," Brianne says, her eyes twinkling with excitement. "I'm not going to be cheesy and overly dramatic. I'm going to be *real*. This is what she wants, right? For someone to pay attention to her story? I can do that!"

"People are going to be cheering and eating hot dogs. Pretty sure that's not what Molly wants." As soon as the words leave my lips, I realize it might not have been the best approach.

"Like I said, I got this. I have a plan."

"Unless that plan is saying thanks but no thanks, I don't think it's good enough," Joshua says.

Bri folds her arms over her chest. "So, you agree with Emmie? You guys all think I should turn down the part?" She looks from me to Joshua to Emmie to me. "Did you see how many people auditioned for it? Practically everyone!"

Her voice is shrill now. I knew this would happen. A few

months ago, Bri and I got into an argument over something dumb. She was upset for a week about it, long after I'd forgotten. Mom said that Bri wears her heart on her sleeve. I didn't know what that meant before, but I think I do now. If Bri is upset, she's going to show it. And judging by how red her face is right now, she's not just upset—she's mad.

Emmie pats her on the knee. "We did see how many people auditioned, and we're so impressed. This is huge, Bri. But this isn't just about you."

"It *is* about me," she snaps. "It's about me finally getting a chance to show what I can do. What if this were a big opportunity for you, Em? Huh? What if this was a photography job? Or you, Mallory? And Joshua...don't act like you wouldn't go after this if it had something to do with painting." She pauses, the hurt in her eyes breaking me in two. "You guys don't think I can do it."

"That's not it." I try to sound confident, but it doesn't come out that way.

Bri's eyes flash with anger. "Forget it. You don't take me seriously. It's why you didn't include me in your little meetings about Molly to begin with. I don't know why I expect you to now."

She stands up.

"I gotta go. They probably want the new cast to meet up for a few minutes before class," she says, taking one final look back before walking out the door. There's a single tear running down her cheek. She sniffs and wipes it away. "I've always done stuff for you guys. I've gone to your photography shows and looked over your projects. It sucks that you can't do that for me even one time."

"Bri, wait," I call out, but it's too late. She's already gone. I sink back down on my rock, feeling heartbroken.

"I'll go after her," Emmie offers. She hops up and runs out the door.

Joshua is still standing awkwardly in the middle of the room. "Is there anything I can do? I feel like I made things worse. Like I shouldn't have even been here when you guys talked to her."

"You didn't do anything wrong."

"Want me to stay here with you?"

I shake my head. "It's okay. Go to class. I'll see you later. I just need to be alone for a few minutes. Okay?"

He nods and leaves without another word. I like that. If he were my mom, he'd ask ten more questions instead of just letting it go.

I shift into a new position on my rock. It definitely wasn't made for people to sit on, because the entire left side of my butt is numb. Scanning the area, I look for something else I could sit on. Something less...sharp. There's a cradle, a papier-maché tree, a ladder, and a paint can nearby. My eyes stop on the paint can, on the bright red paint that has dried where it dripped down the sides.

My blood turns to ice. That color is familiar. Too familiar.

Rushing over, I try to open the lid. It's stuck. I dig out my house keys and use one to pry the metal up. When it finally lifts, I gasp. I was right. The bloodred paint pooled inside looks just like the color of the jagged, dripping letters on my bathroom mirror. I pull my camera up and scroll back to the picture I took that day, confirming it. This is the same paint that showed up on the mirror in my house. That means Molly has been here! I do another quick look around the space, confused. Why would she come backstage? There's nothing but props back here. My eyes land on the large piece of wood propped up next to the paint can. It reads *The Merriweather* in ornate script. Ugh. They must be planning on putting that on the boat they'll use in the festival.

I put the lid back on the paint, a sinking sensation filling me. Molly came backstage for a reason, and I don't think it was to hang out with a bunch of fake rocks. This paint can is another clue, maybe the biggest one of all.

THIRTY-THREE

She's standing on the rocks again. Molly. Her stringy hair twists in the wind, and the tattered scraps of her gown cling to her bony body. I try to reach her, to ask what she wants from me, but I can't. No matter how many steps I take, she stays rooted in the same spot, and I never close the gap.

Behind her, the fog clears, revealing the harbor. It's a sea of Sweet Molly–themed clothing. Tourists. They're lined up on the docks, their faces a mix of excitement and anticipation. A bright light shoots into the air with a bang. I try to muffle the sound with my hands, but everyone else cheers.

A large ship comes around the bend. The plaque on the front of it reads The Merriweather. It sails past. A boy waves from the front of the boat. The applause is deafening now. Confetti shoots into the air then sprinkles down like orange and black rain. The boat turns slowly, leaving the harbor and heading out into open waters.

As the Merriweather drifts into the distance, a band begins to play. That's when I see Brianne. She's walking toward the harbor, her body draped entirely in white. The path along Gaunt Street clears for her, the observers forming a tunnel as they wave and clap and celebrate.

Molly looks at me from the rocks, her eyes black with fury.

She turns toward the cheering masses and points a finger.

Within moments, everything is swallowed by a cloud of darkness. The wind kicks up the ocean, turning the waves into a froth of whitecaps. The docks shudder and people begin falling in. I watch in horror as the water tosses their bodies around like rag dolls.

Brianne drops to her knees and clutches her throat. She can't breathe! Instead of helping her, the crowd does the same. They fall down in unison, their faces turning an unsightly shade of blue as they sputter like old engines.

I want to save them, but it's too late. I can't breathe either. I wheeze and cough, falling down on the jagged rocks.

Molly just watches me. Her lips curl into a smile.

It's over. It's all over.

~~~

I wake up screaming. My hair is matted to my forehead with

sweat. I suck in gulps of air, grateful to be able to breathe again. When I finally feel like I'm no longer suffocating, I look around and try to orient myself.

I'm in science class.

Everyone is staring at me. Emmie is on her feet, but I think I hear someone tell her to sit down. There's a hand on my shoulder.

"Are you okay? Mallory?"

The voice finally registers. It's my teacher. I look up at her and force myself to nod.

"I'm okay," I croak. There's no point in trying to explain what just happened. I fell asleep during class and Molly took over my dreams.

Mrs. Alberti looks less than convinced. "Oh dear. You're shaking and pale. Are you sure you don't need to see the nurse?"

I try to sit up straighter. Look more alert.

Clearing my throat, I answer. "No. I'm good."

A sharp pain in my knee makes me look down. A spot of crimson blooms through my jeans in the exact same spot I remember falling on the rocks in my nightmare. I cross my legs, hoping no one notices.

"If you're sure. If you need to, please feel free to go in the hall and get some water or just catch some fresh air." She moves back to the front of the classroom and picks up her book again.

Slowly, my classmates begin to look away. They're whispering though. I would too. That was weird, even for me. I exchange a glance with Emmie, one that hopefully says *we're in bigger trouble than we thought*. Then I look over to where Bri is sitting. Her eyes meet mine for a split second before flicking away. She has no idea. No clue that her dream role is about to turn into a nightmare, not just for her but for the entire town.

We can't let that happen. We have to stop this.

THIRTY-FOUR

So, Molly is planning to hijack the anniversary celebration and kill us all unless we can get it canceled. Wild, huh?

Nope. Can't say it like that.

Turns out there's no good way to tell your friends that a spirit is planning to overthrow the town. I've practiced at least ten different ways of saying it in my head, and they all sound the same. Awful.

By the time the final bell rings, I'm a nervous wreck. Mostly because I know what we have to do now, and it's going to be nearly impossible. Harder than bathing a cat, as my grandma would say. Plus, Bri still hasn't spoken to me. To any of us. I have no idea how I'm going to fix things with her.

The nausea bubbling in my stomach returns.

I'm finally in the library with Joshua and Emmie. The

sky outside has darkened, and the wind has started up again. Leaves whip around in the air like they're caught in a cyclone. I watch them spin and whirl until they finally fall and plaster themselves to the damp pavement.

"Spill it. What happened in science?" Emmie says, her bright eyes fixed on me like I'm the last bag of Flamin' Hot Cheetos at a 7-Eleven. "I texted you like a dozen times today and you didn't answer. You're lucky I didn't leave class and hunt you down."

She would too.

"It was another nightmare," I say, my mouth going dry when I think about what I saw. "Like the ones I was having before, only worse."

"Are you okay?" Joshua asks. "I was hoping we were done with those."

I laugh sarcastically. "Well, apparently not, because this one was a doozy."

I know I'll need to tell them more about the dream, and I will, but I don't feel ready yet. Just thinking about it makes me feel like I'm going to puke. Or worse, pass out and make a fool of myself again. This time in front of Joshua.

Instead, I turn on my camera and angle the viewing screen toward her and Joshua. "You know how I wanted to stay behind when we were backstage?"

Emmie and Joshua nod and lean in.

"Well check this out." I point at the picture. "Recognize the color?"

"Looks like OPI Red," Emmie says. When Joshua shoots her a baffled look, she adds, "What? It's my favorite nail color."

I frown at her. "Um, no. I was thinking it looks exactly like the color of the message Molly wrote on my bathroom mirror."

Joshua's jaw drops. "Whoa. It definitely does. Do you think Molly used this paint? Like went backstage and got it?"

"Pfft. Ghosts are magical. Molly wouldn't need to steal paint to use on Mallory's mirror," Emmie scoffs.

"Exactly!" I answer excitedly. "What I mean is, yes, I'm convinced Molly used that exact paint. And Emmie, no. I don't think she *needed* to steal it, I think she *wanted* to. It's another clue."

When neither of them say anything, I continue. "The paint can is backstage with all of the props for the anniversary celebration. It was sitting right next to a sign they made for the boat they're using as the *Merriweather*. I don't think that's a coincidence. I think the two are connected."

Joshua is nodding slowly. "Well, we already knew that Molly is angry about how Eastport uses her. Are you saying you think it's specifically the anniversary celebration that's making her mad?"

"I think that's what's making her act out more right now, yeah."

Emmie perks up. "Ooh! Like Goob when he doesn't nap. He gets super cranky and melts down even more than usual."

"Sorta?" I say, laughing despite how bad the day has been.

"But wait. Why *this* celebration?" Emmie continues. "Doesn't it seem a little weird that after all these years and all these parades, this one would bother Molly so much?"

"Good point," Joshua chimes in, quickly glancing around to make sure no one is listening in. "I've lived here for three years, which is a *lot* of parades. Why would this one bother her when the others didn't?"

Good thing I spent all of math class working this out in my head. I'll likely fail my next test on probability, but at least I should be able to convince Emmie and Joshua that I'm right.

"You're right. There have been a lot of parades. But this one is unique. It's the first one to focus on Liam." I set my phone down in front of them. The screen is open to the City Council website. "Check this out. I found it during history."

"Archived events," Emmie reads out loud. The librarian gives her a look. Not quite a *shut up* look because librarians are nice, but more of a *calm down* look, probably because Emmie does talk loud when she's excited. "What does that mean?"

"It's a list of past events that they've hosted here in Eastport." Using my finger, I scroll down the list. "Each listing is a link too, so you can click on it and pull up pictures of the event."

Sweet Molly Parade on Gaunt.

Sweet Molly Parade on Gaunt.

Sweet Molly Parade on Gaunt.

Sweet Molly Reenactment in town square.

Sweet Molly Parade on Gaunt.

Sweet Molly Parade on Gaunt.

Sweet Molly Dramatization.

"See a theme?" I ask. "Besides the fact that there are too many parades in this town?"

"It's all Molly," Joshua answers without missing a beat. "Every single one is about Molly."

"Bingo. Think about it. The anniversary celebration is different. It's about Liam. A Harbor Point student is going to play Molly's brother in the reenactment. He'll sail away from the dock as hundreds, maybe *thousands*, of people watch. They'll cheer and eat churros and wave their balloon animals. They'll act like the worst day in Molly's entire life is something to celebrate."

My insides twist at the thought.

"That's...*horrible*," Emmie finally says. "I never really thought about it that way."

Joshua looks stunned. "It makes sense. If Molly's spirit has been trapped here all this time because she can't find peace, this event definitely could have triggered her to become angrier. To target us." He gestures between himself and me. "We're newer and less into the legends than everyone else here. We're her best chance at making some real change, and she knows it."

I'm so happy I could cry. They get it. Now I just gotta get them on board with the plan.

"I'm glad you guys agree, because what I'm about to say isn't going to be fun. Or easy." I think about how Brianne reacted to our suggestion earlier and wince. This plan is going to get a reaction from the town that is much, *much* worse. "We need to stop the anniversary celebration. The parade, the party, all of it."

"Gah. I knew you were going to say that." Joshua flattens his lips into a tight line, clearly bothered. "Even if that is what Molly wants, how would we do that? Getting this festival canceled is going to be like trying to stop Halloween itself."

"No, it will probably be worse," I mutter.

Emmie is shaking her head. "Doesn't matter because it's not gonna happen. Look at what went down when I tried to tell everyone the real history behind the Eastport Inn! Look at how Brianne acted when we tried to get her to give up the role! They don't want to hear this stuff, guys. They don't want to know the truth."

"We can't give them a choice. The truth is the only thing that will fix all of this. I'm convinced of it."

"I hate to ask this, but... What if we fail?" Joshua levels

a serious look in my direction. "Do you think Molly could do something bad if we can't get the celebration canceled? Something dangerous?"

I think about the nightmare. About the feeling of suffocating, and the way Bri looked when she dropped to her knees. Yes, Molly could do something dangerous. In fact, I think she's planning to unless we stop this. She's had enough, and I don't blame her.

"Yeah. I do. The nightmare I had when I fell asleep during science was more like a...vision? It showed me *exactly* what will happen if we don't stop the festival." I lick my dry lips, feeling anxious. "It was bad, guys."

"How bad?" Emmie asks. She's absentmindedly uncurling the wire from one of her notebooks. It's a nervous habit she's had forever. By the end of the year, half of her notebooks will be nothing but a stack of papers held together with binder clips.

"Death and destruction bad." I swallow back my unease. If I want them to do this, if I really want Emmie and Joshua to help me get this festival canceled, then they need to know what I saw. "The nightmare showed a huge storm and people falling into the ocean and suffocating and—"

Joshua holds a hand up to stop me. His face is ashen. "I had that feeling too, remember? The calm before the storm feeling? I didn't know a real storm was coming but—"

"But we've been connected since the beginning, so this makes sense," I finish for him. "Our dreams. Our sleepwalking. And now this."

So, it's not all made up. The curses. Maybe Eastport really is the most cursed town in the USA, and they just don't know it, I think.

"Now you see why we need to get this event canceled," I say grimly.

"Well, I'm all in," Joshua says. "Whatever it takes. Like you said, no choice. Em? You in?"

Emmie nods, but her expression is uncertain.

I take her hand off the wire of her notebook and try to curl it back into place. "I know it's scary. You don't have to do this if you don't want to."

Even as I tell her this, I know it isn't fully true. We need Emmie. *I* need Emmie.

"I want to help. I do. It's just so much more serious than anything I've investigated before. I mean, this isn't something that could just get us grounded or get our phones taken away. This could get us *killed*."

Her words send a fresh wave of fear rippling through me. She's right. This isn't a game, and if we lose, the stakes are higher than they've ever been.

"I know," I finally answer. "But if we don't try to stop this, who will?"

After what seems like an eternity, Emmie meets my gaze. "No one."

"Does that mean you're in?" I ask, silently begging the universe for her to say yes. Emmie might be nervous about this, but when she makes her mind up to do something, she gets it done. Every. Single. Time.

"I'm in."

I pump a fist in the air, then snatch some paper out of Emmie's notebook and start making a list.

Project Reverse the Curse is officially a go.

THIRTY-FIVE

"Okay. We only have five days until the festival." Emmie shows us a calendar on her phone screen. "That doesn't give us much time."

I nod in agreement. "True. But I have a plan. *And* we have an in."

Joshua swings his head in my direction, his eyes widened in alarm. "Please tell me you aren't thinking what I think you're thinking."

"Just hear me out. She's our only chance, Joshua. Out of the people on the city council, your mom is the only one who might actually listen to us." I pause, hoping his expression will switch from *deer in the headlights* to *I get it and I'm still on board*.

He exhales loudly. "We can try. But how are we going to convince her? I don't even know how to start explaining this."

"That's the problem. We can't explain it," Emmie says definitively. "If we tell them what we know, they'll shut down. I've tried. We need a different reason."

Other than an alien invasion, I can't imagine a reason big enough to make this town cancel the festival.

"Anyone have an idea?" I ask. "Anything?"

A phone dings. I look down at mine even though I don't recognize the sound.

"That was mine." Joshua swipes at his screen. His eyes brighten. "Whoa. Weird coincidence. That was my mom."

Something about his tone makes me think it wasn't an ordinary text. People don't look as shocked as he does when they get texts about boring things like homework or dinner.

"Please come to my office ASAP," he reads. "I need to talk to you about the anniversary celebration. It's important."

When Joshua looks up from his phone screen, I see something new in his expression. *Hope.*

"She never asks me to come to her office. Do... Do you think it's canceled?"

My heart speeds up. This could be huge.

"She didn't say anything else?" Emmie says. "Nothing more specific?"

"Nope. But she said it's important." Joshua stands up and puts his coat on, then swipes his backpack from the floor.

"I don't think she'd send me a text like that if it was about balloons or something."

I grab my things and follow him to the door. "Can we come with you?"

"For sure. Let's go."

I glance back at Emmie, suddenly realizing she's not next to me. "Em? C'mon."

She slowly picks up her coat. "I'm coming. I'm coming."

Oh no. Emmie wouldn't be taking her time like this if she was as excited as Joshua and me. And if she's not excited, that means she's thinking something totally different than us.

"You don't think this is good?" I ask her.

She zips her coat and shrugs. "Maybe. I mean, it could be. I just don't know why she'd call Joshua and make him come to her office to tell him the celebration is canceled."

My hope fizzles.

"I do," Joshua says, motioning for us to walk through the door he's holding open. "There's an auction portion of the event. I'm supposed to be donating two watercolor paintings for it. She would definitely want to tell me in person if the event is canceled and I did all that work for nothing."

"See?" I say, jabbing Emmie gently in the side. "That makes sense!"

She reluctantly smiles and blocks my next poke. "Okay! Okay. Stop."

I frown. "You're still making that face."

"What face?"

"The *stop getting excited, you fools* face."

Emmie laughs as she pulls a hood up over her waterfall of hair. Red tendrils spring out everywhere, framing her face. "Fine. I'll be optimistic. For you."

I wish she hadn't added that *for you* on. I take a deep breath of the chilly air, telling myself not to let it spoil my mood. No one can be right all the time. Even Emmie. I tell myself this is one of the times she's going to be wrong.

The main entrance of the school looks different than it did when we came in this morning. The large arched doorway is covered with fake spiders. They look like they're crawling every which way, trying to find a way in. The railings to the steps are shrouded in ribbons—orange and black, of course—and a large banner with a picture of the *Merriweather* on it is hanging nearby. Even the swing sets in the little kid parks are lined with ribbons and dangly rubber skeletons.

Who decorates a park for little kids that way?

I stop, noticing the large black clouds moving in. They're so ominous they look fake. A distant groan sends the hairs on the back of my neck into a standing position. Everything looks just a little bit darker than it did a while ago. Like Eastport is being swallowed up by something. I don't like it.

As soon as we're inside the city council building, Joshua begins leading us through corridor after corridor. Every door has a nameplate on it. I pause when I see Mr. Hibble's. I imagine him laughing at our fears, his rotund frame shaking beneath another ugly Eastport shirt.

"Joshua?" A voice stops me in my tracks. Joshua's mother has rounded the corner just ahead of us. She looks shocked. "Goodness, you got here quickly! And you brought Mallory, I see."

"Yeah." He sticks a thumb out toward Emmie. "And this is Emmie."

Emmie extends her hand for a handshake. That made my dad laugh the first time he met her. Guess he didn't expect someone wearing a T-shirt with a giant taco on it to be so formal.

Joshua's mom smiles. "Lovely to meet you, Emmie." She turns back to her son. "Why don't you three come into my office, hmm? I have some cookies that a colleague brought in."

"Okay." Joshua's voice cracks, giving away his nerves. He immediately clears his throat.

She leads us around the corner to a door at the end of the next hallway. I notice that the walls are covered with black-and-white pictures, all of various Eastport parades. There's even one picture that looks like it was taken with a drone. Hundreds of people are arranged in a pattern that spells out *Molly* in huge letters. I look away.

She opens her office door and gestures for us to sit down. There are two armchairs and a small couch. And yes, there are cookies—pumpkin shaped, of course. If my stomach didn't feel like it's turning inside out, I'd eat one.

"I called you here because I have some news I think will put a smile on that face of yours!"

Emmie gives me a side-eyed look. I know what she's thinking. Why would Joshua's mom think the event being canceled would put a smile on his face? I force the thought out. This could still be big. We need it to be big.

Joshua tenses in his chair. "What is it?"

She grins. It reminds me of the Cheshire Cat in *Alice in Wonderland*. All teeth. Lots of trouble. Maybe this isn't going to be as good as we thought.

"Well, I presume you've heard that they announced the cast for the big reenactment at the festival?" She taps on a folder sitting on her desk. "The council helped make those decisions. It's important that we picked just the right person to play each part. They have to look, act, and feel like their character. Authenticity matters!"

I smother a laugh. There's nothing authentic about what they're creating.

"I'm confused," Joshua says. "What does this have to do with me?"

"Ohh, this has *everything* to do with you." Opening the folder, Joshua's mother begins flipping through the pages. "You see, there's still one cast member that hasn't been announced. One that we took longer to decide on."

"Liam," Emmie whispers. "I saw the cast list after Bri was announced and noticed that they hadn't cast Liam yet. It only said TBD."

To be determined.

The Cheshire Cat smile grows larger. Joshua's mom pulls a page out of her folder, sets it on the desk, and spins it around for us to see. It's a black-and-white photo of Joshua.

He startles back. "What is this? What's going on?"

"They chose *you*, sweetheart. The council and the school think you would make the perfect Liam!" She pulls another page from the file and sets it out next to the picture of Joshua. It's a picture of what looks like a painting. A young man stands at the helm of a ship.

"Is that Liam?" I ask, my mouth flopping open and refusing to stay closed. If I didn't know better, I'd think it was Joshua. The hair. The eyes. Even the tiny smirk on his mouth is identical.

"It is!" She claps her hands. "Isn't it wild? They could be twins!"

A clap of thunder rings out. The lights flicker. I look at the window, at the wind gusting outside. I didn't think it was possible for it to look darker than it did when we came in, but it does.

"So, the festival isn't canceled," Joshua says in a monotone voice.

"Canceled?" she hoots loudly. "Good heavens, no! That would be horrible!"

Right. Horrible.

Joshua's jaw tightens as the lights flicker again. "Why would they choose me for this?"

She waves him off like that fact doesn't matter. "You don't have to be an actor to do this. You're simply going to ride on the front of the boat and sail out into the sunset. Maybe recite a line or two. That's all!"

He stands up and begins pacing. I've never seen Joshua angry before, but I'm guessing this is it. "No."

His mother stiffens. "What do you mean, *no*? No, you don't want to do it? It's a huge opportunity, Joshua!"

"For who?" he shouts, startling me. "Not for me."

She stands and swiftly shuts her door. "Lower your voice this second. The last thing I need is for my colleagues to overhear this and think we're ungrateful." Her gaze tracks to me and Emmie. "Perhaps it's time for your friends to leave so we can discuss this."

Joshua moves in front of the door and crosses his arms over his chest. "I want them here, Mom. They're the only good thing in this place." When her face crumples, he softens his tone. "I get that you want us to fit in here and all, but I don't want to do this. Actually, I don't think anyone should do this. That's what I came to talk to you about."

She stuffs the papers back into the folder and closes it. "Then I'm afraid our conversation is over for now, honey."

"Why would it be over? You moved us here without asking me, you picked out the house without letting me see it... Why can't you just listen to me on this one?"

"Because it's not my choice," she says matter-of-factly. "The mayor handpicked you, Josh."

Rain lashes the window with such a fury I'm afraid the glass might break. The sky is no longer broken up by dark clouds, it's taken over by them. There's nothing but slate gray as far as I can see.

"So?" Panic rises in his voice. "You have to try to convince him not to do this, Mom. You have to tell him this is a bad idea. All of it."

"Tell the mayor of Eastport that the festival he's been planning for months—the festival that will bring more money into this town in a single weekend than in the past year—is a bad idea?" She sounds incredulous.

I'm so frustrated I could scream. We once learned a quote in school: "Those who do not remember the past are condemned to repeat it." Never thought I'd still be thinking about that quote months later, but here I am. Joshua is begging his mother to listen to him, just like Molly begged this town to listen to her. They're making the exact same mistakes they made two hundred years ago when they ignored her and sent Liam out to sea in a storm.

"Besides, saying no to the mayor could mean I don't get reelected next term," Joshua's mother continues. "And if I don't get reelected, your spot at Harbor Point is gone. No job, no tuition."

This is the same thing my father told me about their restaurant. I hate Mom's performances at The Hill, but there's no choice. I have to play along or else. Apparently, so does Joshua.

"So, what are you saying? There's no way out of this?"

"I'm afraid not," she answers, her expression grave. "In five days, you'll be Liam whether you like it or not."

THIRTY-SIX

I'm numb. The feeling is worse than when our compass plan failed. It was bad enough to know that Bri was going to be in this doomed performance. But now Joshua too?

My head is spinning.

The doors of the city council building slam shut behind us. They sound final, like that moment in my nightmare when Molly smiled at me.

It's over. It's all over.

The rain has slowed to a drizzle, but the sky is still dark. It looks more like midnight outside than four thirty.

"I knew it," Emmie says. "I didn't want to be right this time. I really didn't."

Joshua sinks down onto the wet curb. He looks lost. Defeated.

"We won't let it happen." I sit down beside him, grimacing at the dampness that immediately begins soaking through my jeans. "I promise."

He drops his head into his hands. "Why won't she listen to me?"

"Adults never listen." Emmie kicks at the mulch lining the walkway. It scatters across the sidewalk in clumps. "They're not going to cancel the performance because of anything we say. It's time to move on to Plan B."

"Which is?" I ask.

She shrugs.

"Oh god. We don't have one," Joshua nearly wails. "What did you say happened in your nightmare? Suffocating and drowning?"

"And people being sucked into the ocean," I say. Emmie punches me. "Ouch! Jeez. He asked."

"That doesn't mean you have to tell him! Sometimes the truth just isn't the answer!" Emmie suddenly straightens up as if she's been hit with a bolt of lightning. "Omagosh. Why didn't we think of it before?"

I wait for her to tell me what it was we didn't think of before, but instead she begins frantically pacing back and forth. Her red hair catches in the wind and whips around her head as she mutters to herself.

"Is she always like this?" Joshua asks. "Like a Mento in a bottle of Coke?"

"Pretty much."

Emmie stops pacing and looks straight at me. "*The truth is the only thing that will fix all of this*. You said that. Do you remember?"

"I remember her saying it," Joshua chimes in. "Back in the library. Why?"

"Because I think it's the answer. We can't cancel the performance, but we can change it. We can use Joshua and Bri's roles to tell the truth!" Emmie nudges Joshua and I apart so she can sit between us. "Joshua, you need to agree to play Liam, okay? Don't fight your mom on it anymore."

"I would literally rather have a tooth pulled. *Lots* of teeth pulled."

I wince at the idea of a toothless Joshua.

"I know, but we need you to be Liam so you can help us hijack the performance." Emmie smiles mischievously. "Same with Bri."

Joshua's forehead is so wrinkled up he looks like my aunt's shar-pei. "You mean play along."

"Yes! You and Bri will pretend to do everything they want, but on the day of the actual performance, you won't follow their script. You'll follow *ours*."

It's brilliant. My nightmare showed what would happen if the festival took place, but more specifically, what would happen if the *council's version* of the festival took place. If we can pull this off...if we can successfully hijack the performance, our version will be different.

It will be the truth.

Bri is backstage when we find her. She's in the white gown again, but this time her face isn't painted. I push past a group of students wearing bandanas and dragging what looks like an enormous net.

Ugh. A fishing net. That must be for the *Merriweather*.

We stop about ten feet away from Bri. I start to ask who wants to try talking to her first, but they each put a hand on my back and shove me from behind before I can get the words out. I stumble forward, making Bri look up.

If eyes could actually shoot daggers, Joshua and Emmie would be in big trouble right now.

"What are you guys doing here? Backstage is off-limits." Bri's face is stony. This is going to be harder than I thought.

"We wanted to say sorry," I say. "For earlier. Everything we said just came out wrong."

"So, you *weren't* telling me to give up the role?" Bri tilts her head to the side, her mouth downturned. She looks so sad. I hate it.

"No, we were. And we shouldn't have. At least not that way." I sigh. "It's just that Joshua and I... We figured out how all of the clues Molly left fit together."

A cluster of students walk by. I pick up a random scrap of paper on the floor and pretend to be reading it. Bri rolls her eyes and takes it from my hand.

"No one cares what we're saying, Mallory. *Talk*."

"We know what Molly wants us to do," I spit out, afraid she's going to lose her temper again and walk away.

Bri's face is pinched. "What is it?"

"Cancel the performance."

She gasps and I immediately grab her hand. "Please listen. We don't want you to lose your chance to play Molly. But we don't want you to get hurt either. And if you go through with this, you'll be in danger. The whole town will."

I quickly tell her about the nightmare I had. She's white in the face afterward. Whiter than her Sweet Molly gown.

"I don't understand. Why is she doing this to us? We didn't have anything to do with what happened to Liam," Bri sinks down onto one of the fake rocks. "It's not fair."

Emmie and Joshua are at my side now. Emmie lowers down into a crouching position so she's face-level with Bri.

"She doesn't care about being fair anymore. She's mad. She wants revenge for what this town did to her brother."

"What they *keep* doing," Joshua adds. "I think Molly's spirit has always been unhappy. But this festival is like salt in the wound. It's a low blow to celebrate her brother's death."

"Molly is going to destroy everything and everyone in this town if we don't do something, Bri." I hope this gets the point across. I know how hard it is to give things up that you love. I had to give up Chicago. And my school. My friends. But life doesn't always give us the choices we want. All we can do is make the best of things.

Brianne fingers the tattered scraps of her gown sadly. "I was so excited about this. Guess I shouldn't have been, huh?"

"It was still awesome." I smile. "The fact that you got this part. We're proud of you."

She rises from her makeshift seat. "I should go tell them that I'm not going to play Molly."

"Wait," Emmie says tugging her back down. "You might not have to do that."

Bri's eyes brighten. "But Mallory said—"

"I know what she said," Emmie interrupts. "And she's right. But we have a plan. Did you mean what you said before? About being willing to play Molly differently than anyone else had?"

She stares at all of us for a long second, then nods her head. "I did. I want to make Molly happy too."

"Then get a copy of the script and the cast list," Emmie answers, her mouth stretched into a wide, toothy grin. "We have some work to do."

THIRTY-SEVEN

"I'm starving," Bri says, clutching at her stomach. "I didn't have time to get a snack before rehearsal started. Could we swing by the restaurant?"

"Sure," I pull up the hood of my jacket so it covers as much of my face as possible. The wind is roaring through the darkened streets, feeling nearly as bad as a snap from one of Janette's damp dish towels. "But we need to be fast. And quiet. I don't want anyone to overhear us—especially my parents."

"About that," Joshua starts. "Why aren't we telling your parents about this? My mom, I get. She's not going to listen no matter what. But yours might."

I shake my head. "I thought about it. But what if they didn't believe me?"

"Mine definitely wouldn't," Emmie says. "The last time I tried to tell them anything about this town they grounded me."

Bri snickers. "And mine think everything is about a boy now." She mimics her mother's voice, which I've heard enough times to know is painfully high-pitched. "*Now, Brianne. If you want to get that boy's attention, making up wild stories isn't the way to do it.*"

A laugh bursts out of Joshua, startling us all. "Like anyone would make up a story like *this* to get attention."

I try to imagine how my parents would react. Part of me thinks they'd listen and actually try to help. But the other part of me, the more rational part, knows how bananas all of this sounds. I don't even think *I'd* believe it if someone told me.

"Besides all that, if we did tell our parents, they could ruin our plan." I slow to a stop. The Hill is just across the street. I squint to see through the window, breathing a sigh of relief when I see it isn't busy.

"So, we're in agreement?" Emmie asks. She puts a fist out for us to bump. "We keep this to ourselves?"

"Totally." I bump her fist. Brianne and Joshua do the same. "But what about the rest of the cast? Won't we need to fill them in on what we're planning? Make sure they're on board?"

Brianne blows warm air into her cupped hands. "Nope.

Whoever plays Liam is the only person with actual lines. The rest of our parts are silent."

"Plus, the more people who know about this, the more dangerous it gets," Emmie points out. "If we clue in the whole cast, there's a chance at least one of them will tell their parents. Or a teacher."

That would be bad. We have to do this on our own.

"Um, speaking of Liam," Joshua starts up. "You're looking at him, Bri."

Her eyes fly wide. "*You*? How? Why?"

"He's a dead ringer for Liam," Emmie says. "The mayor picked him."

Bri rolls her eyes. "Wow. So even though you aren't into acting and didn't audition, they gave you the part? That's so wrong! Tons of guys auditioned for that!"

Emmie opens the restaurant door, swatting at one of the dozens of plastic bats hanging from the awning. "Well lucky Joshie here didn't have to jump through those hoops. His pretty face was all it took."

Josh gives her the stink eye. "Haha. I'll remind you guys that we are lucky I did get that role. It's stupid, and I don't want it, but it makes our plan a little easier."

"That's true," I agree with him, then wave to Janette. She's walking toward the back room with a tray filled with waters balanced above her shoulder. I don't even bother trying that anymore. The last time I did it, we ended up with three wet customers and a half dozen broken glasses. "Let's stay in the front. It will be quieter up here."

Just as the words leave my mouth, the sky brightens with a zigzag of lightning. Thunder follows. It's loud and deep, so deep that I feel it in my chest. I look around the restaurant, feeling grateful to be indoors. Candles flicker on the tables, the air smells like cinnamon and coffee, and it's warmer than a toaster. The bell rings in the kitchen and Mom's voice drifts in from the back room. For once, it feels like more than the wacky place where I work. It feels like safety.

We shrug off our coats and take turns sliding into an open booth. I sit furthest on the inside. Joshua sits next to me. I briefly wonder if he did it on purpose, then shake off the idea. Of course, he didn't. Out of the three of them, two had no choice but to sit beside me. He probably didn't even think about it.

Dad emerges from the kitchen. His apron is covered with flour. Ah. No wonder it smells like cinnamon in here. Must be a pie day. "Hey there! I just thinking about you, kiddo. School was good?"

"Yeah. We were just planning to do some homework here if that's okay," I avoid looking at his eyes. Somehow lying seems worse when I do that. "This is Joshua, by the way."

My father extends his hand to shake. "Nice to finally meet you. Sorry I missed you when you were over the other night."

Bri and Emmie look at me questioningly. I shrug. They knew Joshua and I did some research together. I don't know why they're acting like we're getting married now.

"Nice to meet you too. Thanks for letting us hang out here. It's"—he looks back out the window and scowls—"gross out."

"Yeah," Dad answers, folding his broad arms over his chest as he follows Joshua's gaze to the street out front. Rain is coming down so fast now it looks white outside. "Strange that none of this was in the forecast."

I look up from the menu that Janette has slid in front of me. "It wasn't?"

"No, and the weather reporters seemed so confused about it," he says, moving to the side so Janette can fill our water glasses. "I had the news on in the kitchen for a while when we were prepping this morning and they said the forecast showed totally clear skies. Then...this."

"Weird," Bri says around a mouthful of bread. At first, I wonder how she can be eating at a time like this. Then I remember my dad's rolls are really good. They could distract anybody.

"Yeah, weird is right. Apparently, the storms just appeared out of nowhere," Dad finishes, pushing the little bowl of butter packets closer to Brianne.

Appeared out of nowhere. Now that I think about it, there have been a *lot* of storms lately. Since I sleepwalked the first time, actually.

Dad leans over the table like he's going to give me a hug, then abruptly pulls back and winks. Maybe he thinks I'm too old for hugs in front of my friends. I wink back. Later I'll tell him that I'll never be too old for hugs, friends or no friends. I'll also offer to wash dishes after closing. He deserves that. My parents might make me help out with The Hill more often than I'd like, but at least they try to make me happy. That's why I'm at Harbor Point even though we can barely afford it. That's more than I can say for some parents.

As Dad saunters back to the kitchen, I refocus on my friends. "Were you guys thinking what I was thinking just now?"

"If you were thinking that these rolls would be dynamite with honey, then yes!" Brianne says, looking around. "Do you guys have one of those comment card boxes in here?"

I have the urge to snatch the roll from her hand and throw it across the room. "Seriously, Bri? No! That's not what I was thinking. I was talking about the weather."

Emmie drags a notebook from her backpack. I notice that the wire is still in mint condition. Nice. "You thinking it has something to do with Molly?"

"Yes," I tell her. "Joshua had a feeling about storm cells."

"Storm cells," she says flatly. "I don't get it."

"You've heard of the calm before the storm, right? Well, I had a night with no bad dreams, and I told Mallory maybe that's what that was. Then the very next day, she had a nightmare about a terrible storm." Joshua looks at me nervously. "If Mallory's dream was a foreshadowing of what will happen during the anniversary celebration, then maybe all of these smaller storms are... I don't know...the lead-up?"

Understanding dawns on Emmie's face. "Oh, like prefights. My dad watches a lot of boxing and stuff. Before every event, there are a ton of prefights. The main fight is always last."

I cringe at her simile. Thinking of facing Molly as the main fight gives me a terrible feeling. Like the time I finally made it to the end of a *Legend of Zelda* video game and had to keep fighting Ganon. Over and over again he killed me. I hope things don't go like that for us at the anniversary festival.

"If we're right, then that means she's gearing up for Saturday. *Preparing*." My voice comes out flat, robotic.

"Let her prepare," Brianne says. "We will too."

THIRTY-EIGHT

An hour later, and we're stuffed. We're also anxious.

I shove the remainder of my cherry pie away, nerves taking over my stomach. "This is it, then? This is the plan?"

We crowd in to stare at the copy of the script Brianne brought. Really, it's just the Sweet Molly poem, only...edited. Big-time. Thanks to Emmie's multicolored pens, it looks like a rainbow now that we've made our changes.

"Just to make sure I understand, I'll be the only one talking?" Joshua asks. "Like, the success of this whole thing depends on what I say? This is a terrible idea."

I try to keep my face blank even though the idea would scare me too. "It's the only way this will work. Brianne won't have a microphone, but you will. They will expect you to speak your lines from the front of the boat before it leaves the harbor."

"I don't know about this." He runs his hands through his hair. "What if it's not enough? And what if she starts freaking out on us before we even get a chance to do this? For all we know, she'll destroy Eastport the second the sun comes up and she realizes the event is still happening."

"You're forgetting one thing," Brianne says. "She's watching us. She knows what we're up to. I think she'll give us a chance to make this happen."

"A chance. Meaning *one* chance," I say. "We have to get this right the first time. No mistakes. Everything has to go smooth and perfect."

Emmie laughs. "Since when does anything go smooth and perfect?"

Since never.

I run back through the plan in my head, imagining all the different things that could go wrong. *It's terrifying.*

"Look, we have a plan. If we follow it, we'll be okay. Just remember, don't tell anyone who doesn't need to know," Emmie says resolutely.

"And don't. Get. Caught," Joshua adds.

Brianne's face pales. "I'm going to end up in jail."

"You're not going to jail." I pat her hand, hoping it calms her down. "Remember, you're an actress. You can do this."

She straightens her spine and nods.

We take turns snapping a photo of the to-do list we scrawled on the back of the script. I use my camera instead of my phone. There's something comforting about the sound, about the soft click it makes when I press the button. I could listen to that all day.

Emmie hands Joshua the script. "Take a picture of this to be safe. Just in case you lose the original."

Pocketing the paper, he flattens his lips again. Uh-oh. I've decided that's his *I'm worried* look.

"What?" I ask. "Joshua... What's wrong?"

"Nothing is wrong. I was just thinking it might be a good idea if we don't meet as often now. It might look suspicious."

"Won't it look more suspicious if we *don't* hang out?" Emmie questions. "People are already used to seeing us together, you know?"

"There are eyes and ears everywhere," I repeat the words I've heard my mother say dozens of times about this town. What she means is that Eastport is small. And people are nosy. Anything that looks unusual or different could get attention. "I hate to say it, but Joshua might be right. If we get caught sneaking around as a group, *all* of our plans could be jeopardized."

"Exactly. If we stay separate and only one of us gets caught, the rest of us will still be safe to carry out our part of the plan."

Well, that settles it. If we really want to pull this off, we need to do everything we can to make that happen. And right now, *everything* means not seeing each other.

Fear pierces me. This plan is scary no matter what. It's even more scary now that I know we'll all be on our own. That's the one thing I've tried to avoid since day one. Most of the time, my camera makes me feel less afraid. I feel calmer behind the lens. But I won't be able to hide behind it this time. I guess it could be worse; I could be Joshua and have to do the talking.

"We can do this, guys," Brianne says, pulling a warm smile to her face. "She's counting on us."

Ha. That's a nice way to put it. And she's right. Molly is counting on us. But she's also prepared to make us pay if we don't succeed.

A bolt of lightning streaks through the sky, and something glass shatters in the kitchen.

Dad emerges, looking haggard. Stripping off his apron, he balls it up and tosses it behind the counter. "I'm afraid that crash was not part of your mother's dramatic soundtrack. That was me dropping our skull punch bowl."

"Uh-oh. That's one of Mom's favorites, right?" I ask. I never did like the thing since it seems extra gross to ladle red stuff out of a skull, but she loves it. Er, *loved* it.

Dad sighs. "Yup. I'm going to run out real quick and see if I can snag a replacement. It's getting late, so the orders are slow anyway. Can you keep an eye on things up here for a few minutes while I'm gone?"

"Um, I guess so. Where are Mom and Janette?"

"Mom is in the back telling stories, and Janette went home for the night."

Thunder crashes outside, and this time, the lights flicker.

"Honey?" Dad prompts.

I drag my eyes away from the window and the trees swaying outside long enough to nod yes. "Sure. I'll stay here until you get back."

Dad looks relieved. "Thanks, kiddo. Wish me luck!"

As he vanishes out into the building storm, I look at my friends. "You guys should go before the weather gets worse."

Emmie and Brianne scooch across the bench seat and stand.

"You sure? I don't want to just leave you here," Brianne says. "Especially if you're right and these storms are just getting worse."

"I'll stay with her," Joshua answers. "We can walk home together then. It's no big deal."

A mischievous smile lights up Emmie's face. "That's nice of you, Joshua. Super nice. Like extra, extra nice."

I slide my foot from under the table and step on her toe. Emmie hops on the opposite leg, somehow managing to wince and laugh at the same time. "All righty then. I'm out. See you guys..." She stops talking, a more serious expression flashing in her eyes.

"We'll see you at the parade." It sounds so final that saying it makes me shiver.

"See you at the parade," Brianne and Emmie echo.

Then they walk out into the howling wind, and I tell myself they're going to be okay. We're all going to be okay.

THIRTY-NINE

"Are you sure you want to do this? Wait with me, I mean?" I ask Joshua. With Emmie and Bri gone, things feel different. Like the moment you step into an elevator with total strangers. It's too quiet, but I don't really know what to say.

He pats one of the unused ghost-shaped napkins on the head and shrugs. "Yup. They'll probably take a different route home since they live closer than us, anyway, and I don't want to walk the rest of the way alone."

I smirk. "Scared?"

He tosses me a lopsided grin. "Like you aren't."

"*Pffft*. I'm not scared at all. My stomach feels like someone just punched me, and my right eye is twitching, but I'm sure that's all totally random."

Joshua laughs. "Right. Random."

The lights flicker again, this time staying off for a

moment longer than before. I suck in a nervous breath, realizing that it seems quiet in the restaurant. Too quiet.

Standing up, I crane my neck to see into the back room. I glimpse Mom by the wall, her arms outstretched and her eyebrows raised as if she's weaving a true tale of terror. Only she doesn't move. She stays still. Frozen.

The candle on our table blazes higher for a split second before going out. I watch in horror as the candles around us extinguish one at time. Wisps of smoke drift into the air like phantoms, and a final earsplitting clap of thunder plunges the room into darkness.

Joshua grabs my hand. The streetlights outside are lighting up the room enough for me to see his eyes, big and round like twin moons.

"It's happening again," he whispers.

I don't have to ask what he means. Based on the fact that my mom is still frozen in the next room, I know. I also know that if people are freezing in here like they did at the parade, that means Molly is close.

The jingle of the bell above the door makes my heart thump harder. A hunched shadow stands in the entrance, a familiar rattle-rasp echoing through the dark.

Joshua stands and pulls me to my feet. We back away as the shadow takes a step, then another.

A gust of wind slams the door shut. The bell flies off and smacks against the front counter before falling to the ground. Molly's rasping grows louder, her squishy bare feet slapping against the tile as she draws closer. Just when I think she doesn't see us, her head swiftly turns. The orbs of her eyes aren't black this time but white, glowing like we're her target. Her *prey*.

"Run!" I scream, pulling Joshua along as I head for the back room. With no light I stumble over chairs and into tables, stopping when I realize I did exactly what the dumb characters in horror movies do.

I led us into the room with no exit.

Panting, I spin around and press my back against the wall. Even through the dark I can see that everyone is still frozen, their faces twisted in shock. Molly rattle-rasps into the room and fixes her gaze on us once more. Her mouth opens. The wail that comes out is so piercing I drop Joshua's hand to cover my ears. When she finally stops screaming, I give his shoulder a shake to get his attention.

"Don't. Move," I whisper, my voice quaking. Joshua is stiff beside me. His clammy hand finds mine again, squeezing so tight I'm afraid my bones might break.

Suddenly, the light bulbs in the ceiling shatter. Glass rains down on top of our heads. I shake it out of my hair, stopping when the bricks at our backs begin vibrating. Spinning around, I discover a large crack is forming in the wall—the wall that holds in the bodies buried at the graveyard next door. Something moves inside the crack. *A finger*. It wiggles frantically in the sediment until it's poking fully out of the broken brick. Another finger claws out, then another. The fingers keep appearing until they form a whole hand. A very mottled, veiny hand with jagged black nails and oozing open sores.

The hand breaks fully free from the wall to reveal an arm. It snags Joshua's sleeve, pulling him toward the wall. Joshua yelps and tries to wriggle free, but it's no use. The arm is too strong, and more fingers are appearing by the second. Before long there will be dozens of arms, and he'll be dragged into the wall. If Molly gets her wish, maybe forever.

Panicked, I grab a tray from the closest table and bring it down on the arm as hard as I can. I do it again and again. Over and over until the hand finally releases Joshua's sleeve and I can pull him away.

The lights suddenly flip on. I shield my eyes, panting from exhaustion. Joshua is on the floor at my feet. So is...

A rubber Frankenstein monster?

The animatronic decoration is lying facedown, springs and wires of all kinds jutting out from its severed neck. The arms are crushed and bent at odd angles. I look up to the wall. There are no cracks. No fingers or arms, just plain old brick. The tray slips from my hands and clatters to the floor.

Applause rings out from all around us. Men and women jump to their feet, clapping and hooting like they're at a concert.

"Ladies and gentlemen, my daughter Mallory!" My mother sweeps her cape out toward me and grins. It's a huge smile, the smile of someone who doesn't realize I was fighting for my life just now.

I look toward the doorway. It's empty. There's no sign of Molly.

Mom leans and lifts a hand to the side of her mouth as if she's saying something undercover. "That timing was *perfect*! I knew you'd get into this someday, Mallory. I wasn't expecting it to be today, but I'll take it!"

My insides wilt. Mom picks up the Frankenstein and sets him up against the wall. He looks pathetic, all beat-up and broken, but I'm sure she loves it. The spookier the better around here.

I meet Joshua's eyes. They're still twin moons, huge and afraid. I give his hand a gentle squeeze. It's scary enough that Molly plans to take revenge if we don't succeed at the anniversary celebration, but it's even scarier to think that she's still torturing Joshua and I because we're the ones she expects to fix this for her. And if we don't, all of Eastport will pay.

FORTY

I'm sitting on my bed, staring at the strange item splayed out in front of me. It has been three days since my meeting with Joshua, Emmie, and Bri at The Hill. Three days since seeing Molly in the restaurant and beating up the rubber Frankenstein. Three days of waiting. Hoping. Praying that everyone can get their part done. My part is lying here on the bed, but I still have no idea how to use it.

We've texted here and there, but everyone is afraid to say much in case our phones get taken. Having proof of what we've done all written out might not be the smartest move.

I look back down at the last text I got in our group thread. It yesterday and from Joshua.

Just two more days…

Yup, Emmie had said in return. Everyone good?

I'm scared.

That last text—the one from Bri—worried me. I'm scared too. We all are. But Bri is a rule follower through and through. She once confessed that we spilled a chai tea latte on my living room rug to my parents when they didn't even notice the stain to begin with! I'm afraid she's going to freak out and tell someone what we've done...what we're planning.

The text thread went dead after that. None of us knew how to respond. Before Bri's message, you could read through them and think we were talking about the anniversary celebration in general. There is nothing...what's the word...*incriminating*. Then Bri dropped the *I'm scared* bomb and everyone got quiet. We just have to hope she doesn't do anything dumb.

"Knock knock!" My dad's voice filters through my door.

I scramble to cover up the thing on my bed, finally settling on flinging my quilt over it. "Come in."

Dad nudges the door open with his shoe. He's got a brown paper bag in his arms. "Restaurant closed early to prepare everything for this weekend. Can you believe the big event is tomorrow? Your mother is still packaging up the special we'll be selling." He pauses, setting the bag down and pulling a smaller foil-wrapped package from it. "Plagued Pretzels!"

He grins and pushes his salt-and-pepper hair out of his eyes. It's longer than usual, probably because of how much he's been working.

My mouth starts watering the second he opens the tin foil. Smells like cinnamon. I take the pretzel from him, moaning as I sink my teeth into it. There's a cinnamon sugar crust on the outside and the inside is warm and soft. Perfect. I look back down at it, realizing that for one of my parents' inventions, this one is pretty tame.

"I take it that means you approve?" he asks with a hearty smile.

"For sure. It's amazing." I hold it up in the air. "What is it? A haunted house?"

"No. It's a mausoleum! You know, a tomb?"

"Oh, yeah." I set the rest of my pretzel down, then tell myself to stop stalling and get it over with. I might not be able to tell my parents what I'm doing tomorrow, but I can still try to protect them.

"Um, where exactly is the tent you guys will be working in tomorrow?" I try to remember the map of the event that's pinned up near the town square. "I just want to be able to come by when I'm not taking pictures."

His face lights up. "That would be great! The customers would love it too. We'll be on the south side of Gaunt Street."

"How close to the harbor?" I ask, afraid of the answer. The harbor is where all the action happens. It's where Joshua will be reciting his lines, where Emmie will do the *thing* we have planned, and where Bri will go off script. If Molly is going to do something bad, it will be at the harbor. I really don't want my parents there. Or Janette.

"Yes! We got prime real estate for this event. We're the last tent right by the harbor. Perfect, huh?"

I suck down my unease and force a smile. "Mmm-hmm."

Thunder ripples overhead. It sounds like it's moving across the sky, like it's a living, breathing thing. As usual, the lights kick out, leaving us in darkness. I fumble for my phone and turn the light on. Dad does the same.

Dad shakes his head. "Man, this weather just won't let up. I heard we set a new record for this time of year. More rain and more wind than ever."

And more danger than ever.

"Shouldn't they be canceling it?" I ask. "The event? The storms are getting worse."

The lights flicker, then finally come back on. Dad shrugs. "Supposed to be nice tomorrow. Not that the forecasters have been right so far. Plus, you know Eastport. I'm not sure an actual hurricane would keep them from having this party."

Unfortunately, he's right.

Dad gives me a squeeze and heads for the door. "Break a leg tomorrow, kiddo!"

I give him a shaky thumbs-up. If I'm lucky, I'll break something better than a leg. I'll break this entire town and its dumb legends wide open.

FORTY-ONE

I wake up before the sun rises. My phone says it's 5:42. It's pitch black in my room, the timer on my LED lights having turned them off at some point in the night. I sit up slowly, my brain sluggishly trying to remember what woke me up.

A scream. Blinking away the haze, I try to remember if it came from inside the house. I'm almost positive it didn't.

Scrambling to my window, I press my face against the glass. It's just foggy enough to make the harbor look thick and soupy. Through the mist I finally manage to catch a glimpse of something moving. A flash of white.

I snag my camera from the desk and fumble until the lens cap is off. Then I focus it on the harbor and zoom in. Molly! Her back is to me, her gown trailing behind her as she slowly makes her way down the stretch of empty dock. She pivots at the end. Then she looks up.

Right. At. Me.

Molly's mouth opens into the same scream that woke me from my sleep. Lightning flashes, lighting up her bony frame and outstretched hand. Her finger is pointed in my direction.

When the lightning flashes a second time, Molly is gone. I flatten both palms against the cold window and sweep my gaze over every section of the harbor. She's not by the bait shop. Not by the rocks. She's not anywhere. Where is she?

I turn away from the window, freezing as a scraping sound starts up at the door. My mouth goes dry. No. It can't be. I hold my breath and listen hard.

The sound is there, soft like someone gently scratching a fingernail against it. In a matter of seconds, it becomes so loud that it seems like someone trying to claw their way into my room. My doorknob begins to rattle.

I race into my closet and shut the door. Shoving aside the hanging clothes, I press myself flat against the back wall, then pull everything back in front of me until I'm covered..

Just as I'm trying to catch my breath, I hear my bedroom door creak open. Then, footsteps.

Swish thunk. Swish thunk. Swish thunk.

The closet grows cold. I shiver and press a hand to my mouth. She can't know I'm in here. If she figures it out, I'm as good as dead.

A few loud crashes make me jump. I clamp the hand over my mouth even tighter.

Stay quiet, Mallory.

The rattle-rasp is close now. She's outside the closet door. I watch the slats, my eyes widening as one long dirt-encrusted fingernail reaches in. Then another. They scrape along the wood as if they're looking for a place to break through it.

Squeezing my eyes shut tightly, I try to even out my breathing so I don't pass out. I wait for the closet door to burst open, for Molly to reach in and yank me out, but it never happens. When I open my eyes again, the fingers are gone. It's quiet.

FORTY-TWO

The sun is shining.

Shining.

Combined with what happened in my room this morning, I'm positive it's a sign. Molly is watching us. I feel like I could throw up.

Heading toward downtown, I do one final read through of the schedule for the day's events. *Parade, harbor display, goodbye to the* Merriweather. Once the parade begins, it won't be long before everyone realizes something is wrong. Bri will make sure of that. Then Emmie is up. She'll cut the power to the mayor's microphone. And my job is to be absolutely sure that everyone is focused on Liam—er, Joshua—when he starts speaking.

I pull the canvas bag back up over my shoulder and keep the contents securely at my side. Eastport is more Halloween-y than I've ever seen it. Not that I'm surprised. It is the big day, after all. Still. *Every* house is shrouded in skeletons, graves, ghosts, spiders, and even the occasional Sweet Molly scarecrow. The gates surrounding the graveyards are all chained up with signs that read *Closed for Celebration* and every shop I pass looks closed as well.

"Mallory!" Mrs. James appears out of nowhere. She toddles up to me, her normal jack-o'-lantern grin replaced with a scowl. "Did you hear?"

Uh-oh.

"Hear what?" I ask, trying to keep my expression neutral. Maybe it isn't even about us or what we did. I fight the urge to cross my fingers behind my back for luck.

"Rumor has it that all of the special anniversary sweatshirts for the vendors and the volunteers were stolen last night!" She says *stolen* like it's a four-letter word. Here, it practically is. There's not much crime in Eastport. Not against living people, anyway.

I shift awkwardly. "Oh, um. Wow. That's terrible."

Inside, I'm cheering. Brianne did it! Out of the four of us, she had the easiest access to backstage and all the supplies for the cast and crew. So, we asked her to be the one to get rid of the sweatshirts. All 137 of them.

She makes a *tsking* sound and shakes her head somberly.

"Who would do such a thing? They were so beautiful too. I heard that the T-shirt shop worked nonstop to get those created in time. And the illustration was just lovely."

It *wasn't* lovely, but I can't tell her that. Brianne was given a sneak peek of the design for the shirts before we even hatched this plan. They had a ghoulish cartoon version of Sweet Molly in the center, with a poem beneath.

Sweet Molly once lived in Eastport

Sweet Molly once loved the sea

Sweet Molly lost Liam to the shadows

Now Sweet Molly is coming for ye

It's hard not to let my face wrinkle up when I think about it. I finally looked up the word for what Eastport has been doing to Molly with their legends. *Exploiting*. They've been exploiting her and her sadness. The sweatshirts absolutely, 100 percent, had to go.

"I better get going, Mrs. James," I say, lifting my camera up from around my neck. Hopefully if I get her to focus on that, she won't ask me what's in my bag. "I have to get down to Gaunt Street to start taking pre-parade pictures."

"Oh," she waves me away. "Of course, of course. You go, dear. Never mind me. I'm just an old woman with too much time on her hands."

Just as I think I'm in the clear, she calls my name again.

"I hope he liked them, dear! The boy."

At first, I'm lost. Then I remember. The flowers! Mrs. James still thinks the flowers I bought from her shop were for a boy. I immediately think about Joshua. I'd never give him flowers. Shoes, maybe, but not flowers. My cheeks flush at the thought.

"Oh, I see those pink cheeks! I hope that means the arrangement worked and there's love in the air!"

I smile despite my nerves. Mrs. James is kinda goofy, but I like her. It's hard to get mad at her obsession with Eastport when she has never known anything different. Like Emmie and Bri, she probably grew up here. She probably also doesn't know the truth about Molly.

She will. After today, she will.

"Thank you for helping. He loved the flowers."

With a sly smile, she scoots away, the collection of Eastport buttons on her shawl clanking against each other with each step.

I reach the mouth of Gaunt Street just in time to see Joshua walk out of Sinister Snips, the hair salon. I was prepared for him to be in costume, but whoa. His hair has been dusted with something white, making it look musty. His face is painted a very unsettling gray, and there's a darker hue just beneath his cheekbones, so his skin appears sunken. My gaze travels to his vintage clothing, which looks more *Pirates of the Caribbean* than fishing captain. Then again, I don't think the council cares that much about being historically accurate. That's the problem.

Joshua's eyes meet mine for a split second. He doesn't react, doesn't even lift an eyebrow, yet I can tell what he's thinking.

Don't react, Mallory.

Don't let them know we're paying attention to each other.

Too risky.

I quickly glance away and pretend to take a photo of the large inflatable ghost billowing in the breeze outside the salon. When Joshua is finally out of sight, I allow myself to breathe.

So far, I've seen evidence that Bri did her job. Joshua is definitely doing his. The only person I haven't seen today is Emmie. Fortunately, she's also the person I know the best. She'll get her job done or die trying.

Scratch that. It's too macabre.

Emmie will get her job done. End of story.

Weaving in and out of groups waving cotton candy, corn dogs, and tomb-shaped pretzels, I spot my parents' tent near the harbor. Dad is decked out in Eastport gear from head to toe. Mom is right beside him. She's wearing a witch hat and her favorite spiderweb cape. As her voice rises and falls, I wonder if she's telling the coffin story or if she chose a different one to tell when she's not in the restaurant. She pauses and waves at me. Her smile is brilliant. I wave back, my nerves churning.

Hopefully they're proud of me after today. Hopefully they see I did what I did for good reasons. Hopefully it doesn't hurt The Hill or my chance to stay at Harbor Point. I run a finger over the cold metal of my camera, telling myself that no matter what happens, I stood up for Molly. Deep down, I think I might've agreed to this plan even if she wasn't threatening us. Speaking up for people who don't have a voice is important... It's the right thing to do, even if it's hard.

And this is definitely going to be hard.

FORTY-THREE

I'm a shaking mess by the time I finally reach my target—the cluster of rocks I hid behind when Sweet Molly was chasing us. Just like I remembered, there's an open spot in the center of them. It's just hidden enough that it should work.

I need it to work.

Reaching into my bag, I pull out the rectangular box. I lower it down between the rocks, careful to make sure it stays upright. According to the directions that came with it, that's important. Then I stand up and try to act normal while also double-checking to make sure no one is watching me. Sheesh. I have no idea how spies do it. I'd literally be the worst one in all of history.

Once I'm convinced the box is hidden, I pull out the power cord. I connect it to the box and begin slowly unfurling it as I move toward the bait shop. Glancing up, I exhale when I realize no one is watching me. There's too much commotion. A crew is setting up folding chairs around the harbor. A face painter is transforming a child into a vampire. A man is crafting super squeaky balloon animals. A woman is teetering around on stilts.

I don't know what stilts have to do with anything, but I'm grateful for the distraction.

As I feed the long power cord down onto the ground, I kick leaves over it to keep it hidden. I tell myself that even if someone does see me, they probably won't think anything of it. They'll assume I'm a volunteer. I mean, I am. Except I'm supposed to be taking pictures, not setting up a device that I used all my money to rent from a local theater group.

Thank you, Spooky Scary Thespians.

When the cord is fully unraveled, I head for the bait shop door. Like before, it's locked. Looks empty too. Joshua thought they'd close it down for today. Makes sense since basically the entire town is shut down for this event. Now I just need to get inside unnoticed.

I set the end of the power cord on the ledge of the front window, then creep around to the back. There I find a window large enough to shimmy through. It's also hidden enough that maybe, just maybe, I can get in without being seen. I say a silent prayer and push up from the bottom of the frame. At first it doesn't move. I shove harder, panting with excitement when it creaks open. Dirt and flecks of rotting wood fly into my face. I cough and wave them away, then slide the window up as far as it will go. Once it won't move any more, I pause to make sure it won't come tumbling down on my back when I'm crawling through. It stays put.

I take one more look around then lower my bag through the window. Then I heave myself up so that my front half is through. With one more push, I fall headfirst onto the ground. Clambering up, I gently close the window and move to the front window. I can see everything from there. Most importantly, I can see the podium in the center of the dock where the mayor will give his speech. If we're right about how this is going to happen, the mayor will start speaking and at some point, the fake *Merriweather* will drift around the corner. The crowd will *oooh* and *ahhh*. Joshua will be at the front of the boat, outfitted with a wireless microphone. The mayor will begin to read that stupid Sweet Molly poem.

And that's when I create the distraction. We can't allow the mayor—or anyone—to read that poem. The only thing we want people to hear is what Joshua has to say.

If all goes according to plan, Bri will lead all the parade goers straight to the harbor in time to see our version of the harbor display. All she needs to do now that she's already stolen the sweatshirts is stay calm.

I spot Emmie. She's sitting right where she's supposed to—beside the speakers. Her foot is tap, tap, tapping next to the multicolored wires running up to the podium.

Emmie glances at the bait shop window, her eyes widening when she sees me looking at her. Like Joshua, she doesn't wave. She doesn't even flinch. But I'm pretty sure the edges of her lips curl up a teeny-tiny bit, enough to say, *so far so good.*

Lifting the front window, I pull the end of the power cord in and find the closest outlet. Once it's plugged in, I sink down to the ground, breathless. My heart is beating so fast I can hardly think straight. First challenge done.

Just when I think I can finally get on my feet again, there's a voice at the door. A man's voice.

"I'm sure I have some twine in here that will work just fine. Anne was just using it to help string up the banner. Come on in."

I scuttle into the corner behind a big cardboard display shaped like an earthworm. There's a jingling sound, then the clear click of a key sliding into the door. No! I thought this through! I planned! I prepared! Still, the one thing I didn't anticipate is happening.

Someone's coming in.

A deep guffaw is followed by the creak of the door. "Parade kicks off in about twenty. You and Mary have a good spot?"

"Sure do. Never seen Eastport go all out like this." A pause. "I'll tell you what I want to see. I want to see the *Merriweather*. I heard the council paid a pretty penny to rent that boat."

The room slowly begins to darken like it has its own dimmer switch. The men's conversation abruptly cuts off. Curious, I peek around the cardboard. Both men are looking out the window.

"Well, would you look at that," one of them says, scratching his head. "Don't tell me we're about to get another storm. It'll ruin the celebration!"

Storm? My stomach sinks.

"No kidding! Those clouds sure are dark. I better get back to Mary and see if she's heard anything about this weather. Thanks for the twine, Tom."

The two men finally shuffle out and lock the door behind them. Meanwhile, I'm still behind the display, my eyes glued on the dark clouds outside the window. My stomach sinks further. They're coming in fast, faster than normal.

I should've expected this. Nothing is normal about Eastport. On the surface, yeah. It looks like any other small seaside town. But if you look a little closer it's just a big ole mess.

When the coast is finally clear, I shimmy out from my

hiding spot. The room is filled with shadows now—deep, thick shadows that make me feel claustrophobic. I creep over to the window and peek out.

Ho-ly cow.

Everything has taken on a dark, ominous hue. Like nighttime arrived early. Every patch of blue that existed on my walk here is gone, replaced with black angry-looking clouds that tower up into the sky like a temple.

The sea of people gathered around the harbor looks less carefree than they did earlier. They're still waving their glow sticks, wearing their devil horns, and swishing their witch capes, but they're fidgeting. Even Emmie looks nervous. Her body is rigid in the chair, and she keeps looking up at the sky.

A prickle of worry hits me. I need the weather to stay stable. My part of the plan depends on it.

Applause starts up in the crowd, then spreads. It's Mayor Covington. From the headstone-shaped hat on his head to the light-up skull chain dangling from his neck, he's dressed in just as much Eastport gear as Mrs. James. All he needs is a foam finger and he'll be in first place. He waddles up to the microphone, pausing briefly to shake a hand here and there like he's a celebrity.

When he reaches the podium, I see Emmie's foot twitch. She's ready.

Good. I am too. I grip the remote for the black box tighter in my hand.

Just as the mayor taps on the microphone, the wind surges so hard it blows the tombstone off his head. Unfortunately, it blows his hair off too. The stringy black wig jets into the air so quickly he can't do anything but hop up and down, trying to capture it.

Emmie is on her feet now. The wind pushes her small body forward hard enough that she has to briefly anchor herself by holding on to the nearest tree. Ripples of concern are beginning to work their way through the crowd. People are getting out of their chairs, mouths gaping as they stare at the swirling darkness overhead.

"Ladies and gentlemen," Mayor Covington says. His voice booms, making several people cover their ears. "Please take your seats. I assure you that we've looked at the radar carefully and today's weather is slated to be perfect."

I don't think Molly got that memo.

"Thank you, thank you," he says as people hesitantly sit back down. "This is a momentous day, friends! A momentous day for all of us. I'm honored to be here celebrating it with you."

The wind slams into the mayor again, staggering him. He grips the edges of the podium and grunts softly. "Now then. As I was saying, today is a day unlike any other."

Another blast of wind. This time it rips down the banner strung between the trees. It flies backward and collapses in one of the few open spaces available. People are exchanging worried looks, now.

Emmie breaks our pact and peeks at me. She mouths something, but I can't tell what it is. I'm too far away. Sweat begins to bead on my hairline and my face feels flushed. The plan seemed so solid. So foolproof. And now my worst fear is coming true.

FORTY-FOUR

When the mayor starts speaking again, I see it. The tip of the *Merriweather*. It's coming around the corner ahead of schedule.

Here's our chance. Maybe our only one.

But first the boat needs to get just a little bit closer. We figured out the range of the wireless microphone Joshua is wearing and know that the boat must be inside the harbor for it to connect to the speakers.

People are noticing it now. As the *Merriweather* drifts closer, they stand up and point. Balloon animals and glow sticks wave in the air. Mayor Covington turns around and splays his arm out as if he's displaying the boat in a magic trick, as if he made it appear.

"Ladies and gentlemen of Eastport, I present to you the *Merriweather*!" His smile is wide and smug.

The applause is deafening. Everyone is on their feet now, screaming and waving at Joshua, who has appeared at the helm of the boat. He stands with one leg propped up and his chest proudly pushed out. Wind throws his dusty hair into his eyes and billows out the puffy white shirt he's wearing.

The ship has stopped moving and is dropping anchors. The waves toss it from side to side. Hopefully Joshua doesn't get seasick.

"I'd now like to recite a little something we all know and love," Mayor Covington croons into the microphone. It's the poem. He's going to start reading the Sweet Molly poem.

My heart leaps into my throat as I give Emmie the signal. She springs into action, toeing the cord on the ground until it's wrapped around her foot. Then she tugs.

"Sweet Molly once—" Mayor Covington's voice immediately cuts out.

Yes!

He taps the microphone and tries to speak again. When that does nothing, he lifts it from the cradle it's on and examines the sides. A volunteer joins him. It won't be long before they figure out it's unplugged, so I have to move fast.

Looking down at the remote, I locate the green button.

PRESS AND HOLD THE GREEN BUTTON TO DISPENSE, the directions had said.

Here goes nothing. I take a deep breath and push it. Within seconds, the machine I hid begins spewing out thick white fog. It rises from the rocks and begins to spread slowly. The people seated nearby jump from their chairs. Some of them run. I mouth out "sorry" to them through the window even though I know they can't hear me. I don't want to scare them; I just want to create a distraction. If no one can see or hear Mayor Covington, then he won't be able to stop them from listening to Joshua.

Except it's not working. The theater group warned me about this. Used inside, the Fogger 4.0 is perfect. Outside is a whole different story. Even the slightest breeze messes with fake fog just as much as it messes with real fog, I guess.

I watch the fog rise from the rocks and immediately vanish with the wind.

"No!" I'm so frustrated I pound on the glass.

The wind roars again, almost as if it's laughing at me.

I need to find Emmie. She's probably already wondering why the fog hasn't shown up yet. Jumping up, I head for the door. Right before my hand hits the knob, I hear a key, a click, and whoosh. It flies open.

A woman with wild gray hair and steely blue eyes is standing in the doorway. Her mouth is open in surprise, her arms wrapped around something thick and bulky. The banner. She's holding the folded-up banner that fell from the trees.

"Hey! Who are you, and how did you get in here?" She drops the banner onto a table, then looks from the lock on the door to me. "Did you break in? Tom! Tom, get in here quick!"

Fight or flight. I remember learning about it in science. It's the moment when your brain and body have to make the decision about whether or not to stand your ground or run. Right now, I feel like I should run.

I jump from side to side, grateful that my parents made me stay in soccer club when I was little. I was terrible at that sport; never scored even one goal. But I learned how to move fast. Faking to my right, I wait for the woman to follow. As soon as she does, I cut back to my left and run straight out the door.

I'm hiding behind a tree when hands grip my shoulders from behind and spin me around. "Mallory! Are you okay?"

It's Emmie. She leans forward and presses her palms to the tops of her legs, panting.

"I'm okay, but someone saw me." I look back nervously. "And the fog isn't working!"

"I think we might have a bigger problem. Look."

She points in the direction of the *Merriweather*. I follow the line of her finger.

The boat is still anchored near the harbor, but not for long. The waves are pummeling it, making rock from side to side so violently I'm afraid it's going to capsize.

"That doesn't look stable. And why isn't he talking yet?" I ask. "Do you think his microphone won't connect or something?"

Emmie's shoulders jump up and down. "I don't know. I'm honestly not sure he can even stand up right now with the way the boat is moving."

Thunder cracks overhead. I shriek and cover my ears. Emmie does the same.

"What do we do?" she yells.

"I don't know!" I scream over the din.

The sky brightens with a bolt of lightning. Thunder immediately follows. It's so loud this time that multiple people scream.

Tears prick at my eyes. This is all wrong. None of it was supposed to happen this way. I got caught breaking into the bait shop. Joshua is out there on a boat that is fighting to stay anchored. And now the fog machine has completely failed.

A sharp pain starts up behind my eyes. I clench them closed and grit my teeth, but it doesn't stop. Sinking to my knees, I can hear Emmie calling my name. She sounds far away and scared. So, so scared. I try to move my mouth to answer her, but my tongue won't cooperate. All I can do is sink further into the leaves, my brain paralyzed by the vision Molly is forcing into it.

Eastport in ruins. Water runs through the streets. Halloween decorations float through the narrow alleyways and puddle in flooded front lawns. Molly is watching from the top of the lighthouse. She snaps her fingers, and the ocean swells so high it swallows the boat bobbing around in its waves. The Merriweather. *I see Joshua for a split second.*

Then he's gone.

FORTY-FIVE

The pain lets up and my eyes open. Emmie is hovering above me, tearful. "Can you hear me? Mallory?"

"It's her," I choke out. "Molly is doing this."

Another pop of thunder sizzles overhead. Rain begins falling fast and hard. It's a sheet of white, like someone pulled a curtain over Eastport.

Emmie looks around wildly. "Did you see her? Where is she?"

"She's everywhere," I swallow back the tears threatening to fall. "We have to get Joshua off the boat. He's obviously not able to do his part, and I already failed. Forget the plan. Forget everything we thought would work." I level a serious look at her, my heart thrumming so hard it feels like it might explode out of my chest. "Joshua is in danger."

We're *all* in danger, actually.

Emmie helps me to my feet. Chaos is erupting around us. People are bumping into each other and trying to take cover under the trees. Little do they know that the trees aren't going to protect them. Nothing can.

I squint through the rain, barely able to see my parents' tent. The front flap has been closed. They probably did that as soon as the wind started. I can just hear Dad say that he doesn't want the plastic utensils and napkins to blow away. I hope they went back to the restaurant before this rain started.

I hope they're safe.

Refocusing on Emmie, I see my own panic reflected in her eyes. Her red hair is hanging in wet strings around her face, and her mouth is settled into a grim line.

"We can't give up, Em. Not like this. Joshua needs us."

A sob escapes her. "Look around you, Mallory. We're not giving up, we're *losing*."

She spreads her arms out over the scene unfolding. Hundreds of people in soggy clothes are fighting for spots beneath the awnings of the nearby shops. Kids are crying. The muddy ground is littered with glow sticks, popped balloons, and half-eaten Mausoleum Pretzels. The sky is practically strobing. And the wind is worse than ever, howling through the trees like a banshee.

I look back out at the boat again, a sob of my own stuck in my throat. Joshua is out there, scared and alone. I feel like I did when I found out my family was moving to Eastport. Hopeless.

Dentons don't give up. My dad's words run through my head. He's said this to me so many times I almost don't hear him anymore. But this time, I can't *not* hear him. Emmie is right; we're losing. But she's forgetting we can still make a comeback. The underdog always has a chance to win, no matter how small.

"We can only lose if we don't try," I tell Emmie. Her eyes widen as if she realizes what I'm about to do. She reaches for me, but it's too late.

I've already taken off.

I'm running through the wet grass, slipping and sliding as I snake around groups of people huddled together. My feet go out from under me when I hit the wet docks. I fall, grimacing as pain splinters up my backside. Using the handrail, I drag myself to my feet and begin scanning the area for the *Merriweather.*

I can just barely see it through the sheets of rain. It's headed for the harbor. Yes! I'm excited until I realize the boat isn't getting closer. Despite the anchor, Sweet Molly is too strong. The waves are dragging it sideways, toward the lighthouse.

Toward the rocks.

The dock shudders beneath my feet. A large wave sends water crashing up over the wood, soaking my feet.

"Mallory!" Emmie is following me. With her hair pulled upright by the cyclone of wind, she looks like a lit match. "Stop!"

I ignore her and frantically wave my arms over my head. Hopefully Joshua can see me. There's a flash of white through the wind and rain. Joshua. He's waving back. The boat is moving sideways now, drifting past the harbor and toward the jagged rocks at an alarming speed.

The front of the ship slams into one of the docks, smashing the wood as it drags past. Joshua is thrown. He clings to the edge of the ship, both arms gripping the side so he doesn't get thrown overboard.

The *Merriweather* drifts toward the dock I'm standing on, crashing into it with such force that I nearly fall down. Another huge chunk of the wood breaks off, lost in the churning waves.

"Mallory, come back! Please!" Emmie shouts. She tries to follow me onto the dock, but the wood is trembling too hard.

Steadying myself, I put my hands out, palms facing her. "Don't try to come any closer, Em. It's not safe."

"It's not safe for you either," she pleads.

"Maybe not, but Molly targeted *me*, remember?" I remind

her. "She left me clues and used my camera to communicate. I can't let her down."

Wait. *She targeted me.* Out of all the people in Eastport, Molly chose me. Maybe the biggest clue to solving this mystery has never been holes in the sand or paint on my bathroom mirror. Maybe it was me.

I never really thought much about why Molly picked me, but I'm starting to wonder if it's not much different from how I choose things to photograph. Sometimes an object jumps out at me because it just feels different. Like milk dribbling out of a tipped-over glass or a bouquet of flowers with one wilted one hanging off the edge. Maybe I felt different to Molly.

I think back on everything, replaying all my conversations with Joshua about *his* nightmares. At first, I thought it was coincidental that he saw Molly in his dreams too. It wasn't. She targeted him after he moved here. Joshua even said so himself. Then his mother was elected to the council and started planning events—events that just made Molly's problems worse. So, she looked for someone else.

That someone else ended up being me.

My heart gallops like a wild horse. All this time I've been afraid of facing Molly alone. Funny, since that might be the only way to end this once and for all.

Scrambling back off the dock and past Emmie, I skid to

a stop at the podium. Brianne is there now, the bottom half of her white Molly gown blackened with mud. I adjust the microphone and signal to Emmie, who scampers back to the speakers and plugs the cords back in. Instead of letting Emmie take over with Joshua like we'd planned, though, I clear my throat and begin speaking.

"I'm here, Molly," I say, my voice competing with the racket. "I'm here for you. Now you have to be here for me."

Suddenly everything stops. The wind. The rain. The waves and the chaos. Even the boat stops rushing toward the rocks.

Brianne doesn't question what's happening. Instead, she reaches out and takes my hand in hers. This is it. This is my chance to fix things for Sweet Molly...to reverse the course. Taking a deep breath, I begin to recite the Sweet Molly poem. Only I don't recite the poem everyone already knows. I read the new version.

Sweet Molly has a message for Eastport

Money is never the answer, you see

For Liam was a hero to this town

Reverse the course or you'll never be free

The moment I stop reading, a flash of white by the lighthouse catches my eye.

"It's her! Molly!" Someone in the crowd shrieks.

My eyes skip to the lighthouse. Molly is near the rocks again, her pale feet dangling inches off the ground like she's floating.

Brianne squeezes my hand. Emmie has a palm over her mouth and one plastered against her chest. I can't see Joshua, but if I could I bet he'd look just like everyone else—terrified. I hold my breath, waiting to see if the vision Molly showed me, the one of Eastport in ruins, is going to come true.

"I'm sorry, Molly," I say into the microphone. "I'm sorry that no one listened to you. I'm sorry that Liam died. And I'm sorry about all this—" Spreading my hands out over the crowd, I shake my head somberly. "You don't deserve this. Neither did he."

Shrugging my bag off, I dig in it until I find the compass then lift it into the air. "Liam Marshall was a hero. I won't let anyone forget that from now on. I promise."

The compass hums in my hand. It feels warm. Molly's dark eyes land on me like they've done so many times before. Only this time I see a new expression in them, something different.

She slowly raises her hand as if to point at me again. I cringe and hold my breath. Instead of pointing, though, her bony fingers come together in

one...

final...

snap.

FORTY-SIX

SIX MONTHS LATER

The scissors dangle at my side. I can't believe I'm doing this.

A crisp breeze lifts my hair from my shoulders and sprinkles the sidewalk with small, green buds from the trees. Spring is finally here, and Eastport looks different. More alive.

"I'd like to welcome everyone to this very special event," a voice pipes out over the crowd watching me. The mayor. He's standing at the very same podium he stood at back in October, but this time his wig is firmly on his head—thank goodness.

After Molly snapped her fingers at the harbor six months ago, she vanished. Nothing was left but waves, rocks, and a lighthouse that looks a *lot* less spooky than it used to. A strange pang of sadness hits me. I don't miss Molly exactly. I mean, I don't know anyone who would miss being stalked by a ghost. But I do miss the mystery of her. Even though it was scary at the time, working with Joshua, Brianne, and Emmie to find a solution was...fun?

"Here in Eastport, we have fine dining." Mayor Covington gestures at my parents, who are sitting proudly in the front row of folding chairs. "We have wonderful shops." He tips his head to Mrs. James.

"And now," he continues, smiling. "Eastport has this!"

The applause is deafening as Mayor Covington pulls the yellow rope dangling beside the podium. The curtain covering the top of the building falls away, revealing a sign.

Eastport Maritime Museum

Beneath the sign is a logo. The new and improved Eastport logo. My jaw drops. I knew that Joshua was working on it and that it was going to be amazing—like him—but I didn't expect this. It's *incredible.* In the center there's a ship skimming across smooth turquoise waters. There's a man at the helm. When I squint, I can see that he's wearing a compass. *The* compass. Liam!

I glance at Joshua, awestruck. He winks and does a little dance to draw my eyes to his shoes. The same logo is imprinted on the side of a fresh pair of black Converse.

Of course. I lift a foot and tap on the heel of my own shoe to let him know I expect a pair too.

"Please join me in a round of applause for our newly renovated museum and the people who made this possible. Thank you to our fantastic council members."

Joshua beams at his mother. I don't blame him for being proud. Without her, today wouldn't be happening. After the incident at the anniversary celebration, Joshua told her all about our ordeal with Molly, and I guess she decided listening to him is a good idea after all. Together, they came up with the idea for the museum.

And even though I didn't expect it, the town of Eastport was into it. Big-time. Their obsession with Sweet Molly has faded, and things feel different around here, like the whole town finally woke up from a very long strange dream. People are finally celebrating Liam for who he was and what he did, not for the agony his sister went through when he died.

Of course, my parents are still doing their coffin-through-the-wall bit at The Hill, and Eastport still has more graveyards than schools, but still. It's progress!

"And the biggest thank-you of all goes to this young lady right here. Mallory Denton," Mayor Covington continues. My parents stand up and clap so loud that I can feel the blood rushing into my cheeks, staining them pink. "Mallory, you'll never truly know how much this town owes you, but we do. Your perspective opened our eyes and most of all...our hearts.

Would you please do me the honor of cutting the ribbon, and re-opening our museum?"

I nod and, with shaking hands, lift my scissors to the blue ribbon stretched out in front of the door. Emmie jumps out with her camera. I love how confident she looks, how happy she is to be in the spotlight. And this time it isn't because everyone in Eastport is angry with her! Emmie might still do some sleuthing around Eastport, but something tells me that her after today, everything is going to change for her. I bet she'll even snag that spot in the Harbor Point upper school she wants so badly. Hopefully we all do.

I pause and hold the scissors steady while Emmie takes the picture, then snip.

As the ribbon falls away, so do my fears. My frustrations. My resentment. All the bad feelings about being moved to this tiny town on the edge of the ocean are gone, replaced with a sense of belonging. I smile, thinking how hilarious it is that a haunting made me like Eastport, but whatever. It happened, and I'm so, so grateful.

The museum door opens, revealing Brianne. She's wearing a collared shirt that reads *Eastport Maritime Museum, home of hero Liam* and a very formal-looking name tag.

"Welcome everyone. I'm your guide for the day." Her smile is blinding. Finally, my friend gets to be the star in something that doesn't involve crusty white makeup and moaning. It's something bigger, something she deserves.

I move through the door with the mayor, my parents, the council, Joshua and Emmie. Brianne leads us to the first display and my eyes fill with tears.

My photographs. Big, beautiful black-and-white photos cover the wall. One is of the tide rushing over the rocks by the lighthouse. One is of a chipped coffee mug with the old Sweet Molly poem on it. One is of the compass and the bouquet.

But my favorite is the picture of the holes in the sand. Back when I first found them, my entire life was one big hole. I felt like I'd never fit in here and the bad things happening to me were making it worse. Now I realize Molly didn't make anything worse. She saved me just as much as I saved her.

A hand slips into mine...Joshua's hand. I might have imagined this moment once or twice (or a dozen times) before, but it wasn't like this. It was scary and awkward, but this, this feels normal. Like the most broken-in pair of Converse shoes in the world.

Joshua meets my eyes and smiles. I smile back.

Maybe I'm not so cursed after all.

What is one thing Mallory and Joshua
can do to make the spirit terrorizing them happy?

_ _ _ _ _ _ _   _ _ _ _   _ _ _ _ _

USING THE MESSAGE ABOVE, WHAT IS YOUR
PREDICTION FOR WHO THE GHOST IS:

_____

AND WHAT PAGE WERE YOU READING WHEN YOU
MADE THIS PREDICTION?

_____

WHAT OTHER CLUES IN THE BOOK LED YOU TO THIS
PREDICTION?

_____

WERE YOU CORRECT?

_____

A: CHANGE THE POEM

ACKNOWLEDGMENTS

Thank you to the readers who've made me the luckiest author ever.

Thank you to my agent, my editor, my publishing team, and all of Sourcebooks Young Readers for making my dreams a reality.

Thank you to my family, who've helped me to believe in myself.

And thank you to my mother, who I miss very much.

ABOUT THE AUTHOR

Photo © Lindsay Currie

Lindsay lives in Chicago, Illinois with her husband and three kids. She loves coffee, Halloween, Disney World, and things that go bump in the night! She is the author of *Scritch Scratch*, *What Lives in the Woods*, and *The Peculiar Incident on Shady Street*. Visit her online at lindsaycurrie.com